# THE ROOM
## WITH THE
# Second-Best VIEW

## VIRGINIA SMITH

HARVEST HOUSE PUBLISHERS
EUGENE, OREGON

Published in association with Books & Such Management, 52 Mission Circle, Suite 122, PMB 170, Santa Rosa, CA 95409-5370, www.booksandsuch.com.

This is a work of fiction. Names, characters, places, and incidents are products of the author's imagination or are used fictitiously. Any resemblance to actual persons, living or dead, is entirely coincidental.

*Cover by Garborg Design Works*

*Cover illustrations and images © Pink Pueblo, Little Lion / Bigstock*

## THE ROOM WITH THE SECOND-BEST VIEW

Copyright © 2016 by Virginia Smith
Published by Harvest House Publishers
Eugene, Oregon 97402
www.harvesthousepublishers.com

ISBN 978-0-7369-6481-4 (pbk.)
ISBN 978-0-7369-6482-1 (eBook)

Library of Congress Cataloging-in-Publication Data

   Names: Smith, Virginia, 1960- author.
   Title: The room with the second-best view / Virginia Smith.
   Description: Eugene Oregon : Harvest House Publishers, [2016] | Series: Tales from the Goose Creek B&B ; 3
   Identifiers: LCCN 2015051366 (print) | LCCN 2016003834 (ebook) | ISBN 9780736964814 (softcover) | ISBN 9780736964821 ()
   Subjects: LCSH: Bed and breakfast accommodations--Fiction. | City and town life--Kentucky--Fiction.
   Classification: LCC PS3619.M5956 R66 2016 (print) | LCC PS3619.M5956 (ebook) | DDC 813/.6--dc23
   LC record available at http://lccn.loc.gov/2015051366

**Printed in the United States of America**

16 17 18 19 20 21 22 23 24 / BP-CD / 10 9 8 7 6 5 4 3 2 1

# Chapter One

The moment his wife set a steaming bowl of chicken and dumplings on the dinner table, Al Richardson knew she was up to something. He narrowed his eyes and studied her too-casual expression as she scurried to and from the stove to deliver more dishes filled with his favorites. Scattered suspiciously among the green beans were bits of bacon, an ingredient Millie frequently refused to serve, claiming wifely concern for his health. The telltale scents of cinnamon and brown sugar wafted from a bowl of fried apples.

Al straightened his spine against the back of his chair, folded his arms across his chest, and leveled a mistrustful glare on her. "Mildred Richardson, what is the meaning of this?"

She paused in the act of setting a frosty glass of iced tea in front of him to lift a round-eyed stare his way. "It's called supper, dear. We do it every night."

"Not like this, we don't." He waved toward the brimming bowl of plump, delectable dumplings and added an accusation. "Is there lemon cake for dessert?"

His favorite lemon cake was reserved for special events, like anniversaries and Christmas, but occasionally she'd been known to brazenly wield the treat as a tool to accomplish an end of which she knew he would not approve. A powerful weapon indeed. If she whipped out a lemon cake, he might as well throw in the towel—or napkin, in this case—before he even knew the source of the upcoming conflict.

3

"No lemon cake." She seated herself, her expression prim, but before he could heave a relieved sigh she mumbled, "It's coconut cream pie."

"You're shameless." His second-favorite dessert and one she seldom prepared because she insisted he would eat himself into a diabetic coma. He caught her gaze, not bothering to filter the accusation from his tone. "There's a scheme rolling around in that head of yours. Out with it."

Instead, she extended a hand toward his. "Can we at least say the blessing first? It's your turn."

He almost snorted. Another obvious move, a veiled insinuation that her objective enjoyed heavenly approval. Her lips pursed in a prim bow, she bowed her head. Taking her hand, Al cleared his expression for the few seconds it took him to murmur a quick prayer and then resumed his glower.

"Well?" he demanded as he pulled the dumplings toward him. "Explain yourself before the suspense drives my blood pressure any higher."

If thirty-eight years of marriage to the woman seated beside him had taught him anything, it was that Millie refused to be rushed. Whether applying her makeup, stripping paint from the ancient carved banister in the entry hall of the monstrous Victorian-era house they'd purchased, or reading the comic section of the newspaper while he drummed his fingers on the breakfast table, his wife insisted on taking her time. Judging by her imperturbable expression and the slow, methodic way she ladled green beans onto her plate, not even the threat of her husband's rising blood pressure would force her to speak before she was ready. Heaving a sigh, Al served himself an extra-large helping of dumplings. Might as well make the most of the edible bribe.

"Justin is moving out this weekend."

She delivered the information casually, though she knew full well he was aware of their handyman-boarder's schedule. An obvious ploy, one he easily recognized. She'd drop a few seemingly random tidbits of information, skittering madly from topic to topic while he grew dizzy trying to perceive a connection. All the while she'd be building a case, leading up to the final piece of data that tied them all together and revealed her objective.

All right. He'd play along. "On Saturday, I think he said." He scooped a generous portion of fried apples and welcomed the sugary cinnamon aroma with a deep inhale. "That's in three days, in case you're keeping count."

She ignored the statistic. "Violet and I are going to finish painting the back bathroom on Friday."

Another random tidbit. Not the bathroom connected to Justin's room in the front of the house, but the back one. Millie and Violet had worked their way from the front bedroom toward the rear, cleaning, repairing, painting, and decorating as they went. Between the two of them they had stripped enough hideous wallpaper (hideous in Millie's estimation, though most of it looked perfectly fine to him) to smother every wall in Goose Creek.

Fork hovering over a morsel of juicy chicken, she watched him. Apparently a reply was expected.

"Okay." He almost added, *Sounds like a good plan*, but put a dumpling in his mouth instead. Better keep his comments to a minimum until he knew the stakes.

"That gives us three finished bedrooms, each with an *en suite*."

"Mm-hmm." He chewed the delectable dumpling, glad for an excuse to stay silent. Normally he would have corrected her use of the fancy word. Richardsons were plain folk. They used bathrooms, not *en suites*. But just now, the quieter he stayed the better.

She speared the chicken and lifted it to her mouth, pausing long enough to add, "The wedding is in thirty-one days."

Another seemingly unrelated statistic, but he was beginning to see a connection. Nine months ago Justin Hinkle moved in to the upstairs front bedroom in a work-for-rent arrangement with which

Al was perfectly satisfied. During the day the young man performed his handyman work for a growing clientele, while on evenings and between jobs he tended to the gazillion-and-one repairs necessary to ensure that this cataclysm of a house didn't collapse and bury them in decades-old rubble.

This weekend Al and Millie would lose their handyman, who had bought a house with his fiancée, Dr. Susan Jeffries, owner of the Goose Creek Animal Clinic, where Millie worked as a part-time receptionist. He would live alone in the couple's new home until the end of May, readying the place for his bride.

In other words, Al would have to begin paying for repair work again. He stabbed at an apple slice. The reminder of the impending drain upon his retirement funds zapped his patience with his wife's verbal game.

"What are you driving at, Millie?" The words contained more peevish sting than he intended, but he refused to back down. "Tell me and get it over with."

"Well." She set her fork down on the edge of her plate and eyed him with a calm gaze that didn't fool him one bit. He noted the rigid way she held her arms, indicating that her hands were clasped tightly in her lap. "A few of the wedding guests need a place to stay, and of course the closest hotel is twenty miles away. So I thought since we have three perfectly good *en suite* rooms sitting empty—"

"Wait a minute." He stiffened his spine and deepened his glower. "Are you suggesting that we invite complete strangers to stay *here*? With us?"

"We *are* opening a bed-and-breakfast, Albert." She picked up her fork and coolly scooped up a few green beans. "Hosting strangers goes with the territory."

"Not until we retire. That was our deal, Millie." He ducked his head to catch her eye. "You agreed to the timing, remember?"

"Of course I remember. This is only a little early."

"Two years and eight days," Al announced. "I have a countdown on my computer."

She lifted a calm gaze toward him. "It's not like I'm suggesting we put up a sign and start taking reservations. I think of this as kind of a practice run."

"What's to practice? You already know how to make beds and cook breakfast."

Her answer was an exasperated sigh that came out more like a grunt. "I knew you would make an issue out of this. It's not as if you'll be inconvenienced. I'll do all the work. You won't even know they're here."

"I'll know." He cast an irritable glance toward the ceiling. "We'll hear them tromping around up there. Flushing toilets in the middle of the night, waking us at all hours."

Millie loaded her fork with apples. "Besides, it's not like they'll be complete strangers. They're Susan's and Justin's relatives."

"They're strangers to me." Now he sounded petulant, an attitude he detested. A mouthful of beans shut off further whining and gave him a moment to come up with an effective argument.

Truthfully, a few overnight guests didn't sound all that intrusive. He'd be at the office during the day, and they'd probably spend their evenings with the bride and groom. What bothered him was the larger issue. If this practice run turned out well—and knowing his capable wife, it would—Millie would press to do it again. Next time the guests might be relatives of someone at church coming to town for a family reunion. Or a long-lost high school friend who needed a place to stay for a few days during horse racing season. If he agreed to this first intrusion, he could be subjecting himself to any number of strangers parading through his home, eating his food, shattering the peace of his morning coffee routine on the veranda. Before he knew what was happening he'd be the pudgy proprietor of a fully functional bed-and-breakfast, his pants too snug from devouring delicious bribes of cake and pie.

No. Sometimes a man must stand his ground. Stiffen his spine. Put his foot down.

He swallowed and looked Millie directly in the eye. "No."

A split second later he wished he could recall the word. Wrong tone. Wrong tack. An arctic blast invaded the cozy kitchen. Had frost appeared on her eyelashes, he would not have been surprised.

"Pardon me?" She set her fork on the edge of her plate.

A decision lay before him. He could backpedal, try to climb out of the icy hole he'd just stepped into, and attempt to restore marital harmony. No doubt a wiser man would do exactly that. But that would mean conceding the argument, something he was not prepared to do. Time to reveal a bit of that stubborn streak she so often accused him of having.

"We have a plan, Millie. An agreed-upon timeline." He picked up his glass, adopting a casual attitude he did not feel.

"So that's it? I have no say in the matter?"

"You had plenty of say when we bought this place." He waved his tea glass toward the kitchen doorway and the sprawling house beyond. "*We don't need six bedrooms*, I said. *We need room for the children at Christmas*, you said. A deliberately misleading statement, I might add. You wanted to open a bed-and-breakfast all along, a fact that you kept from me."

At least she had the grace to lower her eyes. "I don't see why you have to drag up old arguments that have nothing to do with the current discussion."

"But they do. The timing for the opening of your hotel—"

"Bed-and-breakfast."

He heaved a sigh. "*Bed-and-breakfast*, then. You specified the timing. It was your idea to take our time fixing this place up and then open when we retire. Your plan, not mine. Plans are plans. They shouldn't be changed at the drop of a hat."

For a long moment she studied him, her eyes narrowing as though testing his resolve. Al kept his posture rigid, jutted his chin, and met her gaze.

With a stiff nod, she retrieved her fork. "Fine. Have it your way."

It took a moment for her words to register. Was she really conceding defeat already? He cocked his head, not quite ready to believe her. "Do you mean you agree with me?"

"Not at all. I think you're being a stubborn old poop." She lifted a forkful of green beans and carefully flicked away a piece of bacon. "But I love you, and I don't want to argue with you, so let's just drop it. Eat your dumplings."

Temporarily speechless, Al watched her cut an apple slice neatly in two. He didn't believe her, not for an instant. Oh, not about loving him. They'd been together for too long, lived too much life together, to doubt their love for each another. But he knew his Millie. She possessed a stubborn streak every bit as inflexible as his. This retreat was temporary, a dodge so she could regroup and come up with another approach.

He turned his attention to his plate. Might as well enjoy the dumplings and pie while they lasted.

❋

"You didn't tell him?" The creases in Violet's forehead traveled upward toward steely gray curls peppered with brown.

"That I've already invited Justin's Aunt Lorna to stay?" An uncomfortable flush rose into Millie's cheeks. She'd been so certain that Albert would see the wedding as an opportunity to practice their hosting skills, she'd agreed before asking him. Now she faced the unenviable task of telling her boss that plans had changed and she'd have to find another place for the relatives to stay.

She took a teacup from her best friend's soapy hands, rinsed it, and applied a damp dish towel. "The opportunity never presented itself."

"Hmm." Violet paused in the act of wiping a saucer and assumed the stance of one about to utter a piece of sage wisdom. "*Three things cannot long be hidden: the sun, the moon, and truth.*"

Impressed, Millie asked, "Who said that?"

"Beats me, but it's a fact." She shrugged and plunged the saucer beneath the suds. "Maybe Al will change his mind."

"Maybe." Though she intended to try, Millie didn't hold out much hope of convincing him. He'd seemed adamant. Not only that, but he'd struck a guilty chord with the reminder of her subterfuge concerning their purchase of this house. She returned the dry teacup to its place in the cabinet. "I felt sure the dinner would soften his attitude."

"The way to a man's heart is through his stomach," Violet quoted.

Millie awarded her a sour grimace. "Apparently not."

"The pie was delicious." Violet gave her a sympathetic pat on the arm.

Millie cast a dissatisfied glance toward the remaining two pieces, covered and ready for the fridge. She'd been forced to rescue them from Violet who, after tasting a slice during their ritual Thursday afternoon tea, would have devoured every morsel without restraint. If the evening was as mild as the weatherman promised, Millie and Al could have pie and a cup of decaf on the veranda after supper. Then, when Al was happily satiated with leftover dumplings and pie, she would broach the subject again. Perhaps if she suggested only *one* houseguest, and that one an elderly lady, he'd be more receptive.

When the dishes had been put away and the kitchen table wiped, Violet retrieved her purse from where it dangled on the back of her chair. "One o'clock tomorrow?"

"Better make it two thirty. The celebration committee is meeting down at city hall at one." Millie shook her head as she draped the damp dish towel over the oven handle. Why in the world had she volunteered to serve on the committee planning the ceremony to commemorate Goose Creek's one hundred fiftieth anniversary? The biweekly meetings were boring and never accomplished anything, which she found beyond frustrating. If *she* were the committee chair, she'd—

No. Her days were full enough without the added responsibility. For once in her life she was determined to sit back, let someone else be in charge, and cheerfully do as she was told.

Besides, she had her sights set on a loftier goal.

She helped Violet on with her jacket and opened the back door. "I'll get the last of the sanding done tonight. Painting that bathroom shouldn't take more than an hour or two."

"Then I'll be home in time to watch a couple of episodes of *Dr. Who.*" Violet zipped her zipper all the way up to her chin.

Millie shook her head. "I don't understand what you find so fascinating about that show."

"*By failing to prepare, you are preparing to fail.* Ben Franklin said that." Violet's eyes gleamed. "If a phone box ever appears on my front lawn and a handsome time traveler steps out looking for a companion, I'll be prepared."

Millie stared at her friend, momentarily at a loss. Sometimes the wisest answer was none at all. "I'll see you tomorrow."

She opened the door. Rufus, whom she'd thrust outdoors in an attempt to coerce him into enjoying the spring sunshine, nearly knocked them over charging inside. Apparently the lazy beagle had been hovering, waiting for an opportunity to escape the enforced healthy activity. He scurried between them, nails tapping on the linoleum, and collapsed with a sigh onto his padded doggie cushion in the corner.

"You really are as lazy as Albert says," Millie informed him. Without lifting an eyebrow, he answered with a single languid wag of his tail.

Chuckling, Violet left the house. After the door closed behind her, Millie gave the damp kitchen counter another swipe with the dishrag and then turned to do the same with the table. Violet possessed many fine qualities, bless her, but thoroughness in cleaning was not one of them.

The kitchen finally tidy enough to suit her, Millie headed upstairs to begin sanding the nail holes she'd spackled this morning before breakfast. On the way she ran an admiring hand along the curved banister as she climbed the stairs, pleased with the smooth feel of the gleaming wood. All the effort to strip, sand, and varnish had been worth every aching muscle and broken nail. When guests stepped into the entry hall through the double front doors, their eyes couldn't help but be drawn up the elegant staircase to rest on the pair of vintage button-backed chairs on the first landing, the mahogany arms ornately carved. She paused to pat the puffy upholstery of the nearest chair. One day she would find a spindly-legged table to set between them. Her mind's eye pictured the exact style she sought in order to create a subtle invitation for her guests to pause, rest, and perhaps pick up the book of poetry resting on the table's polished surface. Faulkner, of course. With a velvet ribbon to mark the poem Albert had read to her the day she'd decided to marry him.

The front bedroom, currently occupied by Justin Hinkle, had been the first one she and Violet finished. She paused in the open doorway to sweep an admiring gaze around the interior. Albert insisted on referring to this room as the Humpty Dumpty Room. Her eyes narrowed when they rested on the place where once a hole had gaped in the wall, and she suppressed a shudder at the memory of mold growing inside. The damage had been minimal and the evidence completely eradicated thanks to Justin's exacting work and several coats of sky-blue paint. The subtle pattern of the bedspread she'd found on the sale rack at Walmart lent an air of elegance to the bedroom furniture left—or abandoned, as Albert liked to say—by the house's previous owners. With a happy sigh, Millie withdrew.

Across the hallway stood the second guest room. This was her favorite of the five upstairs bedrooms. Not only was it the largest, but this room boasted two floor-to-ceiling windows that overlooked the tree-covered backyard. Last summer she'd spied a robin's nest cradled in the branches of the nearest sturdy walnut tree just beyond the window, and had come upstairs often to peer through the glass as the mama bird cared for her eggs. The day the eggs hatched, Millie had remained plastered to the window for hours and had successfully recorded the emergence of one scrawny, scraggly baby on her phone. She'd sent the video to five-year-old Abby, who then called to say, "Grammy, that's even uglier than Ursula in *Little Mermaid.*"

In winter, without the covering of leaves, the bare, prickly branches gave a clear view of the pond, where Canada geese would soon begin to nest. From the master bedroom, located directly beneath this one, Millie and Albert enjoyed an unobstructed view and had already identified three distinct pairs.

Music echoed up the stairway, drawing her away from the window. She'd left her cell phone on the kitchen counter. Someday she would ask someone to show her how to select a ringtone for different people so she could tell who was calling without having to see the display. That way she'd know whether or not to dash for the call. At this time of the afternoon, it might be Alison calling from Italy to say goodnight before she went to bed.

Intent on hurrying, Millie hastened down the staircase. Though there was basically zero chance she would make it to the kitchen in time to take the call, something urged her forward. If it *were* her daughter, Millie could call back immediately and hopefully catch her before she silenced her phone for the night.

Hand resting on the banister at the bottom of the staircase, Millie took the last two steps with a hop. The moment the heel of her slipper touched the polished wooden floor, a dreadful certainty seized her. She was going to fall. These adorable fuzzy pink slippers were made for comfort, not for leaping down staircases. Grappling with her right hand, she grabbed the newel post and flailed the air with her left in an attempt to shift her weight to land on the part of her body that possessed the most padding. With a teeth-jarring jolt that sent tears to her eyes, her posterior thudded onto the bottom step. Or maybe the tears weren't the result of the landing so much as the agony that shot up her arm when her right wrist, wedged between the posts, wrenched sideways.

At first she thought the pounding that penetrated the cloud of agony was only in her mind. She identified hurried footsteps as a figure, blurred behind a veil of tears, rushed toward her. Albert's familiar voice sounded in her ears.

"Mildred Richardson, what have you done?"

# Chapter Two

"I t's going to be a small wedding. A few family members in Reverend Hollister's office." Susan smiled at Mrs. Barnes and positioned the stethoscope drum over the cat's left lung.

"Arnold and I were among your first patients." Seated in the only chair in the small exam room, the elderly lady's hands rested on the shiny black pocketbook in her lap. "We almost feel like family."

Susan maintained a pleasant expression, though the urge to laugh nearly overpowered her. On the first day after she bought the Goose Creek Animal Clinic, Mrs. Barnes had nearly ended her career before it began. One minor slipup in referring to Arnold's sixth toe as a mutation—an unfortunate word choice, though entirely accurate—and the sweet little old lady had bristled like a porcupine. She'd called on all her friends to boycott the clinic. Thankfully, Susan had managed to win the approval of enough of Goose Creek's pet owners to keep the clinic afloat.

She kept a gentle hold on Arnold's plump body to keep him from leaping off the metal exam table. The slight wheeze she'd detected in his right lung was more pronounced on this side. A year ago she would have drawn blood and sent it off to the lab, but since moving to Goose Creek, where the feline population nearly equaled the human, she'd become something of an expert in cat maladies. Arnold had feline calicivirus, or possibly herpesvirus. Both infections were prevalent in shelters and multicat homes, and easily transmitted to other cats through sharing food and water bowls, or coughing and sneezing.

As if to prove her point, Arnold sneezed. A fine mist sprayed the metal surface in front of him.

"The poor dear has been doing that for two days," Mrs. Barnes said, tsk-tsking at her pet.

Susan removed the stethoscope from her ears. "How many cats do you have now?"

"Five." Clear blue eyes twinkled. "The baby came from Tootsie Wootsie's litter."

Making a mental note to call Tuesday Love, the owner of Tootsie Wootsie and proprietor of Tuesday's Day Spa to schedule an exam, Susan gave Arnold a final stroke along his spine and lifted him from the table.

Mrs. Barnes stood, looped her pocketbook over her arm, and gathered him up. "What's the matter with my little man?"

"He has an upper respiratory infection." Susan plucked a pen out of her lab coat pocket and picked up Arnold's chart. "We've caught it fairly early, so I think he'll make a full recovery. I'll give you an antibiotic, enough for all your cats. You'll also need to keep them isolated." She glanced up. "They don't go outside, do they?"

"Weeeeelll." She lifted Arnold higher in her arms to nuzzle his furry neck with her chin. "Arnold and Belinda do enjoy an afternoon stroll in the sunshine."

Great. Susan jotted a note on the corner of the chart, a reminder to stock up on antibiotics for the clinic's supply cabinet. "For the next three weeks, please keep them inside. This virus is highly contagious."

She held the door open for Mrs. Barnes and stopped at the medicine cabinet on the way to the reception area to gather enough antibiotic to treat five cats. Thank goodness Arnold was the last patient of the day, and there had not been another feline in the Kuddly Kitty waiting room when he arrived. There went her plans for a relaxing evening at home with Justin. It would take a couple of hours to sanitize the clinic.

Alice Wainright, the afternoon receptionist, took the exam sheet from Susan and began keying the codes into the computer.

"And how's poor Fern, dear?" asked Mrs. Barnes.

Only someone who knew Alice as well as Susan did would have noticed the slight wince at the mention of her oldest daughter's name. *Poor Fern* had turned eighteen several months ago and returned home from the juvenile detention center, where she'd lived since being convicted of theft and possession of methamphetamines. Though Alice was shy and private by nature, she'd revealed enough details for Susan to realize her daughter wasn't readjusting well to small-town life. Especially a small town with an active gossip chain and a penchant for dredging up old news if current events didn't provide something juicy enough to keep them entertained.

Alice flashed a smile that faded as quickly as it appeared. "She's a big help to me with the children, watching them while I work."

Mrs. Barnes's lips tightened and her tone dropped into the disapproving range. "I'm sure she has her hands full with those boys of yours."

The Wainright brothers enjoyed a reputation around town for being rough-and-tumble and more than a little mischievous. Justin referred to the ten- and eleven-year-olds as *high-spirited*. In Susan's opinion they'd crossed the line between impish and delinquency last fall when they strapped a kite on Nina Baker's dog, Pepe, and tied him to Edith Boling's hundred-and-thirty-pound Boomer, for what became known around town as the Flying Chihuahua Caper. Poor Pepe still had to be sedated whenever a breeze blew.

When Mrs. Barnes and Arnold left, Susan twisted the dead bolt and sagged against the door. "Could you do me a favor before you leave? Call Tuesday Love and ask her to bring her cat in for an exam. Tell her not to worry, but I want to check for a feline virus."

"Okay." Alice picked up a note and extended it. "Miss Hinkle

called. She wants you to let her know which florist you've decided
to use."

A familiar pain began in the base of Susan's skull, and she rubbed
a knot that had taken up permanent residence in the back of her neck.
She didn't want to offend her future aunt-in-law, but Aunt Lorna's
phone calls were becoming bothersome. "I've lost count of the times
I've told her we're *not* having flowers. Or music. Or printed invitations." She shoved the note in her pocket, glad once again that she
had not given Aunt Lorna her cell number. She'd return the call later,
from the office phone. "You might want to add disinfectant solution
to the supply list. I'm going to wipe us out cleaning up after Arnold."
She sighed. "It'll probably take all evening."

"Do you want me to send Fern over to help?" A hopeful expression
appeared on Alice's face.

The poor woman had confided her concern over her daughter's
inability to find a job. Creekers possessed long memories, and not
many were forgiving.

Though Susan sympathized with Alice, the few times she'd met
Fern had left her unconvinced of the thoroughness of the girl's reha-
bilitation. She might be completely trustworthy, but why tempt her
with free access to a veterinary clinic, where a variety of medicines
were kept in stock?

"Thanks, but I prefer to do it myself. Otherwise I'll worry about
cross-infections." She flashed a quick grimace. "My control-freakish
tendencies, you know."

She was saved from further discussion when her cell phone rang.
Retrieving it from her pocket, she glanced at the screen and experienced a pleasant rush of warmth at the appearance of her handsome
fiancé's image. With a farewell nod at Alice, she answered the call and
headed toward the privacy of her office.

"Hey you," she said into the phone, using the soft tone she reserved
just for him.

"Hey."

The one word, clipped in a tight tone, told her more than a twenty-minute conversation. She halted and gripped the phone tighter. "What's wrong?"

"It's Millie," Justin said. "She fell down the stairs and is on her way to the hospital."

"Were you there when she fell?"

"No, I pulled into the driveway as Al was helping her to the car."

Car, not ambulance. That was a good sign, anyway.

"I offered to go with them," he continued, "but she said no. Kept insisting she was fine, but I don't think so. She was white as a sheet and hobbling like a cripple. And crying, though she tried to hide it. Al said he'd call as soon as they knew anything."

"Keep me posted, okay? I'll be here at the clinic for another couple of hours."

"I thought you were cooking dinner for me tonight."

"Change of plans." She grimaced, though he couldn't see her expression. "I've got cleanup duty here."

For the first time during the conversation his voice relaxed. "Want some company?"

"If you can operate a mop, I'd love the help."

A low chuckle rumbled deliciously in her ear. "Last time I checked, my mop operator's license hadn't expired."

She smiled. How many men would volunteer to scrub floors just to spend time with their woman? There wasn't a luckier girl in all of Kentucky, of that she was certain.

※

"I'm fine, really."

Al didn't believe her, not for a second. Despite the brave words, tears flowed in rivers down Millie's face to soak the crisp white sheet. She shifted on the hospital bed and sucked in a shuddering breath.

He stood at his wife's bedside, arms resting on the metal rails that kept patients from tumbling to the floor. No danger of that happening to Millie though, when even a slight movement caused a gasp and a fresh flood of tears. "You're obviously not fine."

"I am," she insisted. "I don't know why I can't stop crying."

"Shock," Al intoned in his most gentle tone. "The doctor says it's natural after the body suffers a traumatic experience."

"Traumatic?" Her lower lip protruded. "That's ridiculous. I fell down the stairs and landed on my rump."

"And hurt your arm," he added.

"I'm aware of that," she snapped. "It feels like a dozen tiny pickaxes have embedded themselves in my wrist and are trying to hack their way out." She attempted to roll onto her side and didn't quite suppress a sob. "Why do they make these mattresses so hard?"

Al deemed it the better part of wisdom to treat the question as rhetorical, and held his tongue. In thirty-eight years of marriage he'd rarely seen his sweet-natured wife so irritable. That must mean she was in a lot of pain. A niggling worry erupted in his mind. What if she'd broken her back, or worse, ruptured a kidney? A person could live with one kidney, but what if the fall had damaged her liver? Could a severe fall jar a person's liver loose?

A wave of fear washed over him. What would he do without his Millie? Life would not be worth living. In sudden need of the reassurance of physical contact, he reached for her hand.

"Ow!" She glared at him. "That's my sore wrist."

He snatched his hand away and clasped it with the other behind his back. "I'm sorry. Did I hurt you?"

"No." Her lovely features contorted, the warning sign of the impending renewal of the salty flood. "What if it's broken? How will I finish painting the back bathroom with a broken wrist?"

Al plucked a couple of tissues from the box on the bedside. "The bathroom can wait. There's no hurry."

"B-b-but there *is*." She grasped the tissue with her left hand and covered her face. "You don't know what I've d-d-done."

Alarm buzzed in a distant corner of his mind, immediately overshadowed by concern for his wife. Millie never cried like this. The sight of her overcome with sobs disturbed him at a deep level. Far more than the time she broke his electric razor using it to shave a sweater. More even than when she left the car in neutral and it crashed through the side of Junior Watson's tobacco barn.

He leaned over the rail until his face hovered inches above hers. "Look at me, Mildred Richardson."

A corner of the tissue dipped a fraction, enough for one eye to peek up at him.

"I love you." He allowed the depth of his emotions to creep into his voice, unashamed when it broke like an adolescent boy's. "Whatever you've done, we'll handle it together."

While her sobs did not cease, they did begin to slow. Al waited, more or less patiently, for her composure to return so she could confess what she'd done. His sense of alarm inflated. Whatever it was, he felt sure he wouldn't like it. With Millie in this state he'd be forced to hide his annoyance, swallow his displeasure, and maintain a calm demeanor. He'd probably get ulcers.

The curtain behind him whipped aside and the doctor entered, holding a chart. At least he'd identified himself as a doctor when they arrived at the hospital. He looked more like he might be working on a Boy Scout merit badge.

"Good news, Mrs. Richardson." The young man slapped the folder against his thigh and smiled at Millie. "Nothing's broken."

She succumbed to a fresh wave of sobs. Relief, Al assumed, though he found it hard to tell the difference.

He faced the doctor. "You're sure? You checked everything?" A pause, and he held the doctor's eye. "Her liver's okay?"

The child-pretending-to-be-a-doctor looked startled a moment and then laughed. Al forced himself not to bristle.

"Everything's fine. She's going to have a sore tailbone for a few weeks." He shifted his gaze to Millie. "We'll give you an inflatable donut that'll make sitting more comfortable. And we're going put a brace on that wrist to give the scapholunate time to heal."

Millie blew her nose into the tissue. "The what?"

"The ligament between the two bones in your wrist. The MRI didn't show any tears, but you've sprained it pretty badly. You'll need to wear the brace all the time." He shook a finger as he might to a young child, which set Al's teeth together. "No cheating."

Fretful creases appeared in Millie's forehead. "For how long?"

"Two weeks at a minimum. Possibly as long as six."

"Six weeks!" She turned wide eyes on Al. "I can't be out of commission for six weeks. I have too much to do."

Al opened his mouth to ask what tasks were so important, but the doctor launched into a lecture.

"Mrs. Richardson, the wrist is a complex group of bones, cartilage, and ligaments held in a delicate balance. If an injury like this isn't allowed to heal properly, it could result in long-term pain, stiffness, and swelling." He'd been speaking seriously, but then the patronizing tone returned. "We don't want that, do we?"

"No," she replied, meeker than Al had ever seen her. "We don't."

"Good." He turned to leave, speaking as he exited. "Hang tight until the nurse brings the splint and your discharge papers. Take ibuprofen for pain. Ice the wrist and the tailbone for twenty minutes, four times a day. Oh…" He paused and looked over his shoulder. "You're going to have a nasty bruise on your bottom. Nothing to worry about. It's normal." With a final grin, he disappeared.

Millie scowled after him. "There's nothing normal about a black-and-blue bum."

Reassured that his wife was in no imminent danger, Al returned to his place beside the bed, intent on forcing a full disclosure of whatever information she'd kept from him. "About that thing you mentioned."

"Thing?" She plucked at the sheet and did not meet his eye. "What thing is that?"

He planted his feet. "You know exactly what thing I'm talking about. The thing you haven't told me. The thing you did. Out with it."

To his dismay, tears once again pooled in her eyes and spilled over rims already red with crying. He plucked another tissue and handed it to her.

"It's just that—" Her voice cut off with a squeak. She swallowed and tried again. "I know you don't want the wedding guests staying at our house, b-b- She drew in a breath and finished the sentence on a sob. "But I already invited them!"

Now the weeping returned in earnest. While Millie blubbered, Al concentrated on drawing deep, cleansing breaths through his nose and passing her the occasional fresh tissue when the others became soggy.

How could she invite people into their home without asking him first? The dumplings and pie proved that she knew he would not approve, and yet she'd done it anyway. He'd been deceived. Manipulated. Played for a sucker by his own wife.

He opened his mouth to voice his outrage, but closed it again. She had a heart of gold, his Millie. He could almost see the way this situation must have come about. Dr. Susan, who was not only Millie's boss but also something of a substitute daughter since their own lived in another country, was planning a wedding. What woman didn't relish weddings? Suppose one day at work Dr. Susan voiced concern that there was no place for her relatives to stay. Softhearted Millie would immediately have wanted to fix the problem. A fixer-upper—that described Millie perfectly. Since she had the means to help, she would have volunteered without thinking twice.

Inhaling a final deep breath, Al laid a hand—extra softly—on her shoulder. She looked up at him, misery plain on her blotchy features.

"If you've invited them, then they're welcome in our home."

His swift capitulation must have stunned her. The weeping halted mid-sob. "Do you mean it?"

"I do. We'll receive them with open arms." He glanced down at her injured wrist. "Or I will. You can receive them with open *arm*."

"But the upstairs bathroom—"

He laid a finger across her mouth. "I will paint the upstairs bathroom." Bending low over the bed railing, he removed his finger to brush a featherlight kiss across her lips. "We are a team, Mildred Richardson. Whatever we do, we do it together."

A new flow of tears began. These didn't bother Al in the least, accompanied as they were by Millie's good arm snaking around his neck to pull him more firmly toward the lips he loved to kiss.

# Chapter Three

And after the kitchen and laundry, there's the upstairs bathroom. I got most of the sanding done yesterday before my…" Millie shifted on the inflatable cushion while she searched for a word. She refused to call her fall an *accident* because that sounded like she'd crashed the car. Referring to it as a fall made her sound like a klutz. Everyone in town was probably talking about her clumsy tumble down the stairs. While Millie enjoyed hearing newsy tidbits as much as the next lady Creeker, the idea of being the primary topic of today's gossip rankled.

Seated in his chair at the kitchen table, Albert poured milk on his Cheerios. "Your setback?"

Not bad, though *setback* insinuated some level of failure. "My unfortunate incident," she concluded. There. At least that made her sound more like a hapless victim and less like a graceless bumbler.

"Right." Albert reached across the distance and poured milk into her bowl as well. "So after dishes and clothes, all I need to do is paint that little bathroom, right?"

She awarded him a grateful smile and picked up her spoon with her left hand. He was being so sweet about helping her. He even called his boss and arranged to take a couple of days off work so he could take care of her, which she appreciated more than she could express.

Violet would certainly have stepped in, but more than a few hours' time in the company of her best friend left Millie exhausted.

"There are still a few rough spots to be smoothed over before it's ready to paint," she told him. "I'll point them out."

He paused in the act of picking up his coffee. "Do you think you'll be able to manage the stairs today?"

Though her initial instinct was to bristle, the slight movement when she straightened sent agony shafting up her spine. With a hiss, she changed her position on the inflatable donut, eyes squeezed shut until the pain dulled to a manageable level, and then grimaced at Albert. "Maybe I'll stay downstairs today. You'll be able to see what needs to be done. And Violet will be here this afternoon to help you."

His head shot upward. "What? No!" He shook his head with vigor. "I'm perfectly capable of painting a ten-foot-square bathroom on my own."

"She's been a big help." Millie stepped up to her friend's defense. "And really, she's quite good at taping the edges. After all the painting we've done, we've developed a system."

"You're welcome to return to your system when you can pick up a paintbrush again." Using his spoon like a knife, he sliced through the air between them. "I will cook your meals, dust your furniture, do the laundry, and sweep the floors. I will even paint your bathroom, but I will not subject myself to prolonged exposure to Violet's absurd sayings and clichés."

Despite the stiffness that held her body rigidly hostage, Millie managed a chuckle. "I suppose that is asking a bit much. I'll call her and tell her not to come."

She scooped up a spoonful of cereal with her left hand and raised it slowly. Half of it slopped over the edge before reaching her mouth. With a sigh, she inspected the mess on her nightgown. No doubt within a few weeks she would master the art of left-handed eating. Until then, there would be an increase in the amount of laundry to be washed.

"Oh, and at one o'clock there's a meeting down at city hall. Would you be able to drive me?"

Albert cocked his head and eyed her. "What kind of meeting?"

Millie met his stare with a clear gaze. "The celebration committee. It'll just take about an hour."

"I don't think you should go. The doctor said to take it easy for a few days."

"Oh, pssht." She dismissed his objection out of hand. "It's a meeting, not a marathon. What's the difference between sitting in a chair there and sitting in a chair here?"

"Comfort." He laid his forearm on the table and leaned toward her. "Are you ready to sit on that air cushion in a hard chair for an hour?"

The question made her instantly aware of the tenderness in her nether region. The slightest movement threatened to upset the precarious balance she'd achieved, and as a result her body stiffened to accommodate, causing pronounced discomfort. Ibuprofen took the edge off the pain but did not go so far as to eliminate it. An hour on those hard chairs down at city hall would be miserable.

Even worse, she'd be forced to sit on the donut in public. Certainly not the dignified image she wished to project. Lulu would make crass comments of which no one would approve, but everyone would repeat in whispers all over town.

Millie straightened her neck and replied with as much dignity as one could muster while perched on a rubber cushion with a hole in the center. "All right, then you can go in my place."

Al's eyebrows sprinted toward his hairline. "Absolutely not. I agreed to help you around the house. Attending a meeting with a bunch of women is clearly beyond the boundaries of our agreement."

"But I have an assignment. I've spent hours doing research that needs to be presented this week."

"Send Violet. She'll have the afternoon free since she's not painting."

Millie shook her head. "I don't dare send Violet, not with Lulu

Thacker on the committee. Violet loses all restraint when Lulu's in the room. She can't stand the woman."

"Neither can I." Al folded his arms across his chest. "Make some calls. Find someone else."

"I don't know who else to ask." To her horror, Millie's eyes began to water. She was not a woman who cried often except at movies and weddings. Certainly she was not one of those females who used tears as a tool to get her way. She couldn't stand that sort of manipulative woman. But once the telltale prickle of tears began, she could not hold them back. Maybe it was because of the disabling ache that radiated from her tailbone all the way up to her skull, or the throbbing pain in her wrist, or the embarrassment of knowing she was being discussed over countless breakfast tables this morning. Regardless, she set down her spoon, covered her face with her napkin, and succumbed. Carefully, since any movement hurt.

"Oh, here. There's no call for this." Albert's chair legs scraped across the floor as he pushed away from the table and hurried toward her. An arm encircled her shoulders and applied gentle pressure as he pressed a kiss on her hair. "I didn't realize how important this meeting was to you. Of course I'll do it."

"No." She shook her head and tried to staunch the flow. "Really. You don't have to. I just—it's only—" The words choked in her throat. "I hate promising and then not keeping my word."

"Of course you do." His soothing voice warmed her ear. "That's because you have integrity. Now, stop crying and finish your breakfast. Then I'm going to help you back to bed."

She heaved a mighty sniff. "I don't want to go to bed."

"Then I'll get you a couple of ice packs, and you can sit in my recliner. Come on. Eat up."

Though sitting on an ice pack certainly wasn't an ideal way to spend a Thursday, the idea of doing anything else left her exhausted. The doctor said she would be sorest the first couple of days. Surely by the weekend she'd be able to stand, if not sit, without agony. In the meantime, she ought to enjoy Albert's seldom-seen tender side.

She placed a hand on his cheek. "You really are a kind man, Albert."

A touch of gruffness returned. "Keep it to yourself. I'd hate to have that spread around."

A movement in the corner drew Millie's attention. Rufus heaved himself off the cushion and ambled to the back door. He turned his head and gave her a meaningful look.

Before she could interpret, Albert straightened. "I suppose I have dog duty too."

"Don't forget to take a bag," she said as he reached for the knob.

With an aggrieved sigh, he snatched a doggie cleanup bag from the box near the door. "Come on, mutt."

When the door closed behind them, Millie picked up her coffee. About forcing Albert to care for Rufus, at least, Millie didn't feel guilty. Spending time together would be good for them both.

※

At one o'clock on Thursday, Al parked his car in front of city hall. Empty parking spaces stretched along both sides of the railroad track that divided Goose Creek's Main Street, which gave the place a vacant, ghost-town-like air. On Saturdays the town bustled with activity. He found the sight of the deserted street more than a little disturbing. Was it always this empty during the week when he was at the office in Lexington?

As he exited his car, Al scanned the buildings up and down the street. Many had been constructed close to two centuries before, and looked it. Crumbling facades, faded or paint-encrusted woodwork, bricks missing or broken. Nearly a third boasted For Sale or For Rent signs in their windows. He shook his head. What made Millie think anyone would want to stay in a bed-and-breakfast here?

On the other hand, a few of the buildings had undergone

renovations. The drugstore, for instance. And the day spa down on the far corner. His gaze was drawn there, to the newly painted trim, the neat rows of pressure-cleaned brick, and the brightly striped awning. Purple wouldn't have been his first choice for the woodwork, but Justin had put a lot of work into transforming that building exactly into what Ms. Love wanted for her establishment.

He opened the door of city hall—one of the town's original structures that had undergone a major renovation a few years ago—and entered an empty reception area. Following voices that echoed across floor tiles made to look like marble, he headed for a small conference room along the back wall.

Frieda Devall, owner of the Freckled Frog Consignment Shop— an establishment that offered a mishmash of frivolous and expensive doodads of which women were unaccountably fond—fell silent when she caught sight of him. Three heads turned his way while Frieda's eyebrows crashed together above flaring nostrils. "What are you doing here?"

"Courier service," he announced. He set Millie's manila envelope on the table and gave it a shove toward Frieda, who seemed to be in charge by virtue of her seat at the head of the table. "If I'm not welcome, I'm happy to leave." In fact, he would be relieved to escape this duty.

Tuesday Love, a mass of blonde curls waving from an untidy but somehow attractive mop on the top of her head, hopped up and grabbed his arm. "Of *course* you're welcome." She slid out the wooden chair beside hers and tugged him toward it. "This group could use a man's opinion. A little Old Spice to combat all the perfume." She gave a girlish giggle that somehow seemed natural coming from the flighty massage therapist.

Seated opposite Tuesday, Phyllis Bozarth lifted a concerned face up to him. "How is poor Millie?"

Of course the entire town would have heard about Millie's fall. Something as exciting as an injury to one of their own had no doubt made the rounds of Goose Creek's female population within minutes of its happening.

"Sore," he replied as Tuesday shoved him into the chair.

He was saved from elaborating when someone else barged into the room. There was no other way to describe Lulu Thacker's entrance. A thin, angular woman with a set of buck teeth that would have made Secretariat proud, Lulu and her annoying husband had moved to Goose Creek more than a year ago when they bought Al's house. Violet, who lived next door, had still not forgiven Al for the Thacker invasion.

"Sorry I'm late, girlies." Lulu's voice held a high-pitched whine that grated on Al's eardrums. "You wouldn't believe the morning I've had. The coffeemaker got clogged and dumped coffee all over the counter. Then Frankie decided he wanted bacon, even though I had the sausage thawed." Laden with a pair of bulging reusable bags, she dropped one on the floor and plopped the second on the table, tongue still flapping. "Of course whatever my Honey Bun wants, he gets. Especially since I forgot to turn on the dryer last night. Every single pair of his undershorts were wet." She let loose with a laugh—a brash, unnerving assault on the ears that bounced off the walls in the small room.

Al shifted in his chair, wishing devoutly that he were not privy to news of Franklin Thacker's undershorts. Was it not enough that he spent hours every day listening to the man's annoying guffaw from the other side of his cubicle wall at work? And that every Saturday Thacker infringed upon the sanctity of the traditional Creeker watering hole, the soda fountain at Cardwell Drugstore?

"Lookie what I brought." She began pulling jelly jars from her bag and banging them onto the table. Next to her, Phyllis jumped every time a jar hit the wood. "Enough for everyone to take home a couple. Worked on it all day and half the night, and mmm, don't my house smell good?"

Lulu caught sight of Al and squinted to peer at him. "Aren't you supposed to be at work?" Without waiting for an answer, she continued her monologue. "My Frankie never misses a day of work. Not once in more than twenty years. Why, he wouldn't stay home on a workday if they paid him double. Every morning, rain or shine, snow or ice, off to work he goes."

Yes, Al was aware of Thacker's excellent attendance record. He'd been subjected to a boastful narrative on the subject more times than he cared to remember.

"You brought us a present?" Tuesday reached across the table and picked up a jar. "That's so sweet."

Phyllis examined the handwritten label on the jar Lulu slammed down in front of her. "Mustard Marmalade?"

At the head of the conference table, Frieda's nose wrinkled. "I've never heard of mustard in marmalade."

"Be surprised if you had." Lulu folded her empty bag and dropped into her chair. "I invented it myself. I used to glaze hams and chickens with mustard and orange marmalade, and one day I thought, *Why not?* So I whipped up a batch and it was a hit. Frankie likes it so much he spreads it on toast. Or sometimes straight out of the jar, if he thinks I'm not looking." She indulged in another nerve-racking cackle that set Al's teeth together.

"I'm excited to try it," Tuesday said as she stored two jars in a giant multicolored purse that looked like it might have been made out of a bedspread.

Al cast a glance sideways, but the flighty massage therapist seemed entirely sincere. He considered asking if she'd like two more jars. Millie would say that was rude, so he kept his mouth shut. But if a mustard-yellow chicken showed up on his dinner table, he would protest. He would not be able to eat a bite with the mental image of Thacker hiding in a corner to suck down spoonfuls of the stuff.

"Can we get started?" Frieda tapped a fingernail on the table. "I'm losing business every minute my shop is closed."

Business? Al stifled a laugh. If there were customers strolling through the streets waiting for the shops to open, they were doing a great job of staying hidden.

"Returning to our previous discussion," Frieda continued in a take-charge tone, "to plan a decent celebration, we need funding." She turned to Phyllis. "What did the city council say to our request?"

Phyllis, who had served on the city council for two terms, shook her head. "The city's budget is too lean. We spent over an hour trying to find any fund we could trim to try to come up with more money for the celebration. Mayor Selbo did allocate last year's budget surplus to us."

"How much is that?" Tuesday asked.

Phyllis sent an apologetic grimace toward Frieda. "Fifty-eight dollars and twenty-four cents."

Lulu reached into her second bag and pulled out a half-finished afghan, arranged it in her lap, and went to work with a pair of knitting needles. The act was so Millie-like that Al frowned. He would have sworn to any and all that his sweet Millie had nothing whatsoever in common with Thacker's brash wife.

"I still say we should do a fund-raiser," she said. "Kids at our old church did them all the time to pay for mission trips and such."

Frieda planted her elbows on the table with a scowl. "What do you suggest we do? Wash cars?" Her lips twisted. "Paint a sign and send one of us out to US 127 to flag down dirty vehicles?"

"I'll do that," Tuesday volunteered.

Al gave her a sideways look and received a guileless smile in return. Was the woman really unaware of the sarcasm in Frieda's suggestion?

Frieda's lips tightened. "It's undignified. This celebration is about our town, our heritage. The citizens of Goose Creek should be proud enough of our legacy to want to celebrate it in a properly dignified manner. I will not stand by and watch it become a cheap carnival funded by cake walks and rummage sales."

"Cake walks!" Lulu sat up, her expression brightening. "Great idea. My parsnip-and-maple cake is to die for."

The comment elicited a stunned silence from the assembled.

"You can't imagine how good it is," she insisted, needles flying. "My Honey Bun would eat a whole cake in one sitting if I'd let him."

"Anyway," continued Frieda with a hard stare at Lulu, "we need a celebration that demonstrates our civic pride. And to do that, we need money."

Though Al had resolved to remain silent, curiosity got the best of him. He voiced a question. "We have our fall festival every year, and that's always a big hit. Couldn't we combine the two?"

A second silence settled in the room. Lulu became absorbed in her knitting, while Phyllis suddenly began scribbling on a notepad with energy. Beside him, Tuesday shifted to the far side of her chair and began an inspection of her fingernails.

"We've covered that ground before." Ice could have dripped from Frieda's lips as the words left her tongue. "This town was founded in the *spring,* not the fall."

"Well, yes, only—"

She cut him off. "Goose Creek is turning one hundred fifty. Don't you think that deserves special recognition?"

"Of course, but—"

The woman made a show of examining her watch. "If we're going to rehash the same issues previously addressed, then perhaps we should plan for longer meetings."

Phyllis's eyes fluttered closed, and Tuesday groaned.

Feeling like a scolded eight-year-old, Al slumped lower in his chair. "Sorry. I'm only here to deliver something for Millie. No need to rehash anything on my account."

Lulu looked up, a question on her horselike features. "I hope Millie's not sick." Apparently Lulu had not become part of the Goose Creek gossip chain.

"She suffered an…unfortunate incident," he explained.

Further questions were halted by Frieda's loud interruption.

"Since you're here, Al, why don't you tell us what Millie discovered in her research?"

Though he'd been subjected to the celebration committee for less than fifteen minutes, Al had had his fill. His promise to Millie had encompassed the delivery of information and a follow-up report of the discussion when he returned home. He had not agreed to participate.

"I have no idea." He dipped his head toward the manila envelope in the center of the table. "It's in there."

Settling a pair of neon green reading glasses on the bridge of her noise, Frieda retrieved the envelope and slid out a few sheets of paper. The only sound in the room while she scanned the documents was the clicking of Lulu's knitting needles.

"Hmm." A scowl settled over Frieda's features, and then the creases in her forehead gradually cleared. Her second "hmm" contained a note of interest. By the time she uttered a third "hmm," this one accompanied by a nod, the rest of the room was watching her with interest.

"It says here that property owners in Goose Creek may be eligible for grants and tax credits if we commit to an effort toward historic preservation."

"Really?" Phyllis leaned sideways in her chair, neck craned in an attempt to read the paper in Frieda's hand.

"We do have a recognized historic district, you know." Frieda looked up over the top of her glasses. "It extends several blocks on either side of Main."

"I didn't know that." Tuesday turned a grin Al's way. "Imagine. I own a building in the historic district."

Frieda handed the top page to Phyllis, who squinted to read. "I've been on the city council for four years and I don't think we've ever discussed the National Historic Registry. Certainly we've never done anything about it. Does it expire?"

"Not according to Millie's notes." Frieda tapped on the second document. "She says a building or district stays on the Registry until it loses its integrity." She glanced up. "Whatever that means."

"But where does the money come in?" Tuesday asked. "Are we supposed to get a check from the government or something?"

Lulu snorted. "The government doesn't give out money for nothing. There's a catch somewhere."

Though it pained Al to realize, he agreed with the annoying woman.

"No, we have to apply and be approved for the financial benefits," Frieda answered, her voice distracted as she read. "But that's for property owners. I don't see how that's going to help the celebration's funding problem. I wish Millie were here to explain." She flipped to the third page. "Oh, wait. This last bit here is about something called the Main Street Program."

Tuesday giggled. "Sounds like something we ought to know about since our Main Street is kinda run-down."

"It says here if we were part of this Main Street Program, we'd get help from the state to apply for special grants and tax credits and so on."

"So let's join," suggested Lulu. "What's it cost?"

"It doesn't say."

Phyllis asked, "Will Millie be well enough to come to the next meeting?"

Al opened his mouth to answer, but Frieda cut him off. "We can't wait two weeks. This says there's a sizable private grant that will be awarded this September to communities who make a good case for how they'll spend the money. We need to hurry and fill out the application to join the Main Street Program so we'll have a shot at that money. That means we need to put someone in charge. They call it a…" She glanced down and tapped on the paper. "A Main Street Manager. It's usually someone hired by the city council."

Phyllis shook her head. "After the last meeting I can tell you the answer to hiring anyone. We can't afford it."

"Then it'll have to be a volunteer position." Frieda rubbed a hand over her mouth, her gaze unfocused. "I'd volunteer, but with my store I can't carve another minute out of my day."

"Same here." Tuesday rewarded Al with a scowl. "If I turn away a single customer I won't be able to make my loan payment."

Frieda looked at Phyllis, who shook her head. "I have a hard enough time getting off work to come to *these* meetings. Between that and the council work, I can't add anything."

Tuesday straightened. "I know the perfect person." She turned a grin on Al. "You could do it. You're smart, and I'll bet you know all about applying for grants and stuff."

Shocked, Al jerked away from her so hard the chair arm dug into his back. "Me? No way." He raised splayed hands. "I have a job. Besides, now that my wife is down to one hand, my honey-do list just tripled."

"What about Millie?" Phyllis suggested.

Al shook his head with vigor. "Between her job at the animal clinic and getting that mammoth house in working order, she doesn't have time."

"She's already done a lot of the research," Frieda pointed out, gesturing toward the documents. "I'll bet she's already figured out the application process."

"No." He imbued his tone with firmness. "She needs time to recover from her injuries."

Lulu spoke without looking up from her knitting. "I'll do it."

Frieda's eyes widened. Al thought he glimpsed a touch of panic in the gaze that circled the table. "I'm sure you're far too busy, what with your...cooking and knitting and all."

"This?" Lulu raised her woolly project. "I'll have this finished by supper. I just knit to pass the time. And cooking is second nature to me. Takes no time at all." Her equine teeth put in an appearance. "I'd be glad for the job. Give me something to occupy myself while my Honey Bun's at work."

"Well…" Frieda exchanged a glance with Phyllis, who gave an almost imperceptible shrug. "As long as you let this committee review the application before you submit it, I guess that'll be fine."

"Perfect!" Tuesday clapped her hands, a delighted smile on her generous lips. "Congratulations, Ms. Manager."

A pained expression crept over Frieda's face as she gathered the documents. "If you have any questions, call." She slid the papers into the envelope and extended it toward Lulu. "Please be prepared to give a progress report at the next meeting."

"Sure thing." Lulu shoved her knitting and Millie's report in her bag. "I'll bring a treat for everyone. Frankie just loves my marmalade cookies."

As the meeting broke up, Al congratulated himself on a job well done. He'd represented his wife at the meeting and rescued her from an onerous task to boot. Taking the two jars of mustard marmalade Lulu thrust into his hands, he exited city hall. Better tell Millie to avoid the cookies at the next meeting.

# Chapter Four

You gave away my job?"

At Millie's question and recriminating stare, Al's jaw dangled. "You *want* to be the Main Street Manager?"

"Well of course I do." Her free hand slapped at the veranda railing, the other resting in the safety of a sling.

When he'd pulled the car to the end of the long driveway, she had appeared—moving slowly and with great care—to take up a stance near the veranda railing. The questions began as Al rounded the car's front bumper.

Now, standing on the grass with the veranda railing between them, Al could only stare at his wife. Had that tumble down the stairs jarred something loose in her brain?

He made a show of wiggling a finger in his ear to clear it. "Excuse me, but I'm not sure I'm hearing you correctly. Why would you want something else to suck up your time? You're too busy as it is."

Her chest heaved with a loud sigh. "I've spent hours researching the application process and finding out about the benefits and responsibilities. I even went to Frankfort and met with the Heritage Council. I'm the one who discovered the Main Street Program, so the job of managing it rightly belongs to me."

He stared at her, dumbfounded. The poor woman was experiencing delusions. "Last week you told me you did not want to be in charge. I remember the conversation perfectly. We were sitting at the kitchen table, finishing supper, and you said—"

"I know what I said, but this is different."

The conversation replayed in his mind. How could he have misinterpreted *I'm going to sit back and let someone else be in charge?*

"I said I didn't want to run the celebration committee." From her tone, she might have been explaining the difference between a circle and a square to a preschooler. "The Main Street Program is different. It's a job."

"Aha. Now we circle back to the beginning. You have a job. Two, in fact." He waved a hand to encompass the house. "Repairing and decorating this place is a full-time undertaking. And next month you're going to have your first guests. You don't have time to be the Main Street Manager."

"Albert, don't be dense."

The irritable tone, so unlike his sweet Millie, provided further proof that her brain was not functioning normally. Pain had obviously clouded her thinking.

"This job will involve a lot of upfront work, but then it will be easy. It's decorating Main Street for holidays and things like that. I'm quite good at decorating."

"You are," he agreed.

A pretty pout appeared on her lips. "I can't believe you turned down my job without even checking with me."

Al rocked back on the heels of his loafers. At times like this, a husband's responsibility was clear. Calm and placate his wife until logic returned. He'd learned two words long ago that, if used sparingly, went miles toward maintaining marital harmony.

He dropped his head and muttered in a humble tone, "I'm sorry."

A quick upward glance revealed that the words worked their magic. Irritation began to seep from her expression.

"Well." Her rigid lips softened. "You couldn't have known what I wanted. I didn't tell you, did I?"

Had he followed his instincts and pointed that fact out, she would have flared. Angry words would have escalated a simple disagreement into a full-blown argument. So much better to let her come to the realization on her own.

"I was only trying to protect you," he said, using his meekest voice. "I don't want you to take on too much."

A smile, small but encouraging, appeared. "That was very kind of you, Albert."

"That's the husband's responsibility." Bolstered by the softening of her tone, he puffed out his chest and expanded his defense. "We're the defenders of the family. The wife's advocate. We safeguard our loved ones, even when—"

"Albert."

Judging by her sardonic expression, he'd taken the protector thing a bit too far. He ducked his head. "Sorry."

But at least he'd accomplished his goal. Argument avoided. Millie no longer looked like she wanted to bite his head off, and a touch of amusement softened her smile.

"Come on inside and tell me about the meeting," she said. "I made a pot of decaf."

Moving cautiously, she turned toward the door, and Al leaped ahead to open it for her.

"What do you have there?" She pointed toward the jars.

"Mustard marmalade." He wrinkled his nose. "A gift from Lulu."

"Really?" Interest sprang onto her face as she took one of the jars and inspected it. "I've never heard of making marmalade with mustard. I'll bet that would be a good glaze for ham."

The idea of eating ham slathered in Thacker's favorite jam sent a quiver through Al's stomach. He stepped in front of her, drew himself up to his full height, and said in his sternest voice, "Don't even think about it."

❈

Susan disconnected the call and slipped her cell phone into the pocket of her lab coat.

Seated at the reception desk, Alice looked up from the chart she was scribbling on. "How is Millie?"

"Better, she says."

Susan glanced into the Playful Pups waiting room, where Tammy Lockridge sat holding a scruffy mixed breed she'd adopted from the pound yesterday. The dog's terrified shivering was visible even at this distance. In the Kuddly Kitties room, Mrs. Elsimmer awaited her turn with her cat, Bullet, in a travel crate at her feet. Though the woman paged through a magazine, her quick upward glance toward the reception desk told Susan her ears were tuned to their conversation.

Susan turned her back toward the waiting rooms and lowered her voice. "She still can't sit comfortably, but she's practicing using a computer with her left hand. She says she'll be back on Monday. Are you okay covering all day tomorrow too?"

Alice nodded, and then creases appeared in her forehead. "I have one problem, though. Tomorrow there's no school because of a teacher in-service day, and Fern has a job interview at the Bistro at ten o'clock." She cleared her throat, and caution crept over her expression. "Sharon has agreed to watch the girls."

Though she left the question unvoiced, Susan knew what was coming. The younger Wainright girls were sweet children, well-behaved and easily entertained. But the boys? The idea of those two high-spirited miscreants hanging around the clinic held no appeal whatsoever. But what could she say? Alice was doing her a favor by working full days until Millie returned. Business at the animal clinic was steady enough these days that Susan couldn't handle the reception desk and treat her patients as well. Finding a temporary replacement on such short notice was unlikely. She really had no choice.

"Nina Baker isn't on the schedule for tomorrow, is she?"

"No," Alice said quickly, her eyes wide. After the episode with poor Pepe, Nina had treated Alice to such a harsh dressing-down about "those delinquents-in-the-making" that the shy receptionist cried for two days.

"They won't be here all day, will they?"

Alice shook her head. "Only until Fern is out of her interview. And I'll make sure they behave. I promise."

Alice intertwined her fingers on the desk in front of her so she appeared to be pleading. The sight sent a wave of guilt washing through Susan. She wasn't trying to be mean or harsh. And it wasn't as if she disliked Alice's sons. They could actually be kind of charming when they tried. But she had a responsibility to her animal patients and their owners to provide a safe environment.

"I suppose it'll be okay."

Alice relaxed, and she exhaled a soft sigh.

Susan adopted a stern tone. "But keep them away from the lab area and the exam rooms. And make sure they're supervised if they come in contact with any animals."

"They'll be on their best behavior," Alice assured her.

Like that was supposed to be reassuring. The only time those boys behaved was when they were asleep. Was it too much to hope that they'd nap all the way through Fern's interview?

# Chapter Five

In the moment after Millie awoke on Friday, her habitual cheerful first-thought-of-the-morning flitted into her mind. *It's going to be a lovely day!*

Then she reached for the edge of the blanket. A tiny movement, barely more than an inch, but one that brought the memory of her injuries crashing through her brain with the weight of a freight train.

"*Ow*!" Tears stung her still-closed eyes. "Ow, ow, *ouch!*"

"Wha—" On his side of the bed, Albert stirred, his voice heavy with sleep. "Whasswrong? Y'k?"

"No, I'm not okay." The sharp pain that resulted from the unwise movement of her sprained wrist dulled to an ache, and her lower back throbbed miserably. "I can't move."

Albert jerked upright, jostling the mattress so that she hissed with pain. "What, are you paralyzed?"

"Of course I'm not paralyzed," she snapped. "If I were, I wouldn't be in this much pain." She gave her voice over to a full-fledged whine. "I hurt! I thought it would be better today, not worse."

"That's probably normal." He stretched, yawning. "Sore muscles are always worse the second day. Everyone knows that."

"Well, someone might have warned me." She regretted the uncharitable snipe and went on in a kinder tone. "Would you help me get up?"

He swung his feet to the floor and rounded the bed, rubbing his eyes. Through the discomfort of her sore spine, Millie spared a smile for his spiky morning hair and rumpled pajamas. Seeing her normally neat husband looking unkempt and charmingly boyish was one of the privileges of marriage that she cherished. In the early days she'd insisted on slipping out of bed before he woke so she could rush to the bathroom, comb her hair, and wash her face. What a relief it had been to settle into the comfortable assurance that his affection for her was not dependent upon her appearance.

With Albert's help, amid much hissing and moaning, she managed to attain a sitting position on the edge of the mattress. Then she had to rest a minute, waiting for the pain to dull and her racing heart to slow, while directing him to retrieve her clothes. A loose housedress today, something easy to put on and not tight around her sore nether region. The slip-on sneakers she typically wore while painting, which had the benefit of being rubber-soled. The idea of applying makeup one-handed was too tiresome to consider, and unnecessary besides. She wasn't going anywhere.

Albert ran a brush through her hair and then stepped back to examine his handiwork. "There. Ready to face the day."

Turning—slowly—Millie caught sight of herself in the vanity mirror and cringed. She touched one pale cheek and then ran the fingers of her good hand through lifeless locks. "I look like a flash-flood survivor."

"Not true." Albert pressed a kiss on her forehead. "You look beautiful to me."

She turned a grateful smile up to him. "Since you're the only one who'll see me today, that's all that matters."

※

The doorbell rang as Millie scooped the last bite of Cheerios from her bowl. She cast a startled glance toward Albert.

"Whoever it is, I'll get rid of them." He rose from his chair, shoved a crust of toast in his mouth, and left the kitchen, brushing his hands on his trousers.

Millie stood and, one-handed, began taking the dishes to the sink while straining to hear the conversation at the other end of the house.

A moment later, there was no need to strain. A voice, loud and blaring, echoed through the hallway and dining room to invade the silence of the kitchen. No question as to the identity of their visitor. Lulu Thacker.

"You know what they say," the woman boomed, "beware neighbors bearing gifts. Though we aren't exactly neighbors, are we?"

Gifts? Millie set her coffee mug in the sink, listening to the rumble of Albert's quiet reply without being able to make out his words.

"I'm not gonna stay long. Just want to pick her brain a bit."

Albert said something, followed by Lulu's, "Oh, don't worry about that. I'm a calming visitor—everybody says so. Wow. Would you look at this place?"

She sounded closer, as though she'd come inside the house. Millie heard footsteps on the hardwood in the entry hall. Albert had let her in.

A long whistle reached the kitchen. "Mighty grand place you got here. No wonder you sold the old house to us. It's a cracker box compared to this here one."

The footsteps continued to grow louder, and now Albert's words were discernible.

"Nothing boxlike about that house. We loved living there." He sounded defensive and a bit remorseful, as he was wont to do whenever he spoke of their old home on Mulberry Avenue.

"Yeah, but you gotta admit it ain't the Taj Mahal. More like the cottage of the Seven Dwarves."

Her hee-hawing laugh blared from nearby. They were in the dining room and heading this way. With a quick attempt to fluff her hair with her fingers, Millie turned toward the doorway. If only she'd thought to put on a hat, as she sometimes did to protect her hair from paint splatter. And a bit of lipstick to give her face some color.

Lulu appeared in the entrance holding a cake pan covered in foil. A grin widened her large mouth to an impossible width. "There she is!" She halted just inside the kitchen. The smile faded and concern descended over her features. "Girlie, you look awful. Are you in that much pain?"

Behind her, Albert splayed his hands in a helpless gesture and shrugged, while Millie forced herself not to react to the rude comment. *Calming visitor my foot!*

"Not at all," she lied. "I'm just a bit stiff."

"Looks more than a bit stiff." Lulu nodded at the sling. "What happened, anyway? I trotted over to Violet's house last night to ask, but she didn't answer the door. Musta forgot to turn her lights off while she went out, 'cause they were on in the living room." She *tsk*ed, shaking her head. "That's the goingest girl I ever did see. Never home when I come calling. I declare, you'd think we lived next to a vacant house for all we see of her."

Poor Violet, reduced to hovering behind drawn curtains to avoid her annoying neighbor. Millie dared not look directly at Albert, who appeared to be trying to control a laugh.

"She's here a lot," Millie said to give her friend an easy excuse. "She and I have done the lion's share of the restoration and decorating in the upstairs bedrooms."

"Well good for you. I don't know one end of a hammer from the other myself. Good thing my Frankie is handy around the house. Oh." She lifted the pan. "I brought you a cake."

Now Albert's eyes went wide with alarm. Millie kept her expression pleasant. "How nice. Thank you."

Lulu stalked to the table and set the gift down. "I figured you wouldn't be doing much baking since you're down to one wing." She whipped the foil cover off with a flourish. "It's a parsnip cake."

Behind her, Albert's chin dropped to his chest.

Millie examined the cake, dismayed. What should one say when gifted with a parsnip cake? "I've…never heard of such a thing."

Lulu indulged in a horselike guffaw and even slapped her thigh. "The look on your face! Girlie, you'd think I was trying to force wet grass down your throat. Try a piece, would you?" She turned to look at Albert. "You too, Bertie. Grab a couple of plates."

Albert managed to look both highly offended at the nickname and appalled at the suggestion that he eat parsnip cake. Shaking his head, he held up a hand. "I just finished breakfast. Couldn't eat another bite."

Lulu shrugged. "Leaves more for us." She faced Millie again. "Tell me where the plates are, and we'll have a little after-breakfast snack."

Though the urge to refuse was strong, decorum won out. When receiving a gift, even an unwelcome one, a Southern lady must accept graciously. Millie smiled and gestured toward an empty chair at the table. "Please sit down, and I'll get the cake knife. Would you like coffee?"

"What's cake without coffee?" She scooted out a chair and plopped into it.

Assuming that meant yes, Millie retrieved her mug from the sink and a clean one from the cabinet. When she made a gingerly movement toward the dessert plates, careful not to jar the muscles in her lower back, Albert came to the rescue.

"I'll do it." He pointed toward her chair. "You sit."

Actually, standing was far more comfortable than sitting, but she couldn't very well let her guest sit while she hovered above her. She lowered herself into her chair, careful to situate the donut in the most advantageous position.

Lulu watched with obvious interest and then jerked a nod toward the cushion. "Hemorrhoids?"

Millie's head snapped up. "No!"

"She had an *unfortunate incident*." Albert set a full coffee mug in front of each of them. "Fell down the stairs," he added, and Millie shot a stern look his way. Must he provide details?

"Don't you have something to do?" she asked through tight lips.

"In fact, I do." He raised his nose high in an attitude of dignity. "I have a bed to make. I'll leave you two to your cake."

Setting the glass plates and a cake knife on the table, he made a hasty exit. Because Millie knew him well, she recognized the relief in his hurried step.

"Bruised your bum, did you?" Lulu reached for the sugar bowl, which was filled with artificial sweetener, and dumped a huge spoonful into her coffee. "Same thing happened to my Honey Bun once. I spilled a bit of vegetable oil on the bathroom floor. Before I could clean it up he came running in 'cause he always waits till the last minute. Hit that oil and *bam*." She slapped one hand down on the other. "Down he went. Let me tell you, his rump turned six different shades of purple."

Torn between the urge to ask what Lulu was doing with cooking oil in the bathroom and the desire to direct the conversation away from any further discussion of bruised derrieres—hers *or* Franklin's—Millie raised her coffee mug to her mouth and changed the subject.

"Congratulations on becoming the Main Street Manager." Though an equally painful topic, at least that one was far less humiliating.

"Thanks." Lulu reached into her handbag and pulled out a crumpled manila envelope. "That's another reason I'm here. I was hoping you could clue me in on this program, and what Goose Creek needs to do to get some of that grant money. After all the work you've done, I'd hate to mess it up."

She extracted three sheets of paper, which Millie recognized as her report to the celebration committee. Millie couldn't help but preen a bit. At least she was being consulted.

"I'm sure you wouldn't mess it up." She awarded Lulu a kind smile.

"I might." Lulu glanced over her shoulder and then leaned close. "I'm not the best at talking to people. Seem to rub folks the wrong way, though I don't know why. In fact, I haven't made a real friend yet here in Goose Creek. That's why I volunteered for the job. Figure if I do something good for the town, folks will get friendlier. But after reading your stuff"—she flapped the papers in the air—"I realized

I'm gonna have to talk to the city council, and Goose Creek business owners, and even the folks over in Frankfort."

Compassion for the brash woman stirred in Millie's soft heart. How distressing, to know one wasn't liked by those she tried to befriend. At least Lulu was aware of her weaknesses. According to Albert, her husband was clueless.

Could she swallow her pride and assist Lulu in the job she wanted for herself?

She covered Lulu's hand. "I think we're going to make a good team. I'm quite good at talking to people."

A huge grin spread across the woman's face. "That's what I hoped you'd say." She leaned back in her chair and picked up her mug. "With my brains and your way with people, we'll make this thing work."

If they were closer, Millie might point out that some would take offense at the suggestion that she had no brains, but since their friendship was still tender, she ignored the slight.

"All right, let's get down to business." She took the papers from Lulu's unresisting hands and spread them out on the table.

Lulu stopped her. "First things first. You're gonna try this cake, girlie."

Millie eyed the gift and allowed doubt to seep into her tone. "Does it taste like parsnips?"

The answer was an earsplitting guffaw while Lulu cut a largish square and scooped it onto a plate. "Taste it and see."

While she helped herself to an equal-sized portion, Millie picked up her fork. A dullish white icing and pecans covered the top. Well, pecans were good anyway. She sliced off a small bite, trying to ignore the whitish shreds that could only be parsnips enmeshed in the moist cake. Steeling her stomach against an unpleasant onslaught, she placed the morsel in her mouth.

Her taste buds flared in a festive celebration. Cinnamon and maple formed a delightful union, blending splendidly with the maple butter frosting. And the pecans! The perfect nutty accompaniment.

"This," she said, pointing at the cake with her fork, "is delicious. I want the recipe."

A satisfied smirk on her face, Lulu reached into her handbag and extracted a recipe card. "I knew you would. Everyone does."

❈

"Albert, what are you doing in here?"

Al looked away from the giant flat-screen television in the room Millie referred to as their "private sitting room." In the old plantation days the space had been a ladies' dressing room, located off one side of the master bedroom. The addition of an indoor bathroom a number of years after the house was built reduced the size of the original dressing room to half. The remaining area had just enough space for Al's recliner, Millie's wingback chair, a bookshelf stuffed with her favorite books, and the television that had been a Christmas gift from the kids a few years before. Though he knew it irritated his wife, Al referred to the room as "the TV closet."

He faced Millie, who stood in the doorway connecting the TV closet to their bedroom. Her lips formed the tight, pinched arrangement he recognized as Millie's version of disapproval. A list of possible infractions flitted through his head.

He had forgotten to take a doggie cleanup bag out this morning when Rufus took his morning stroll. Well, perhaps that lapse had been a result of selective memory, because he found it demeaning to follow the pooch around the yard. She may have discovered that offense.

Or perhaps the bedspread and decorative pillows were not placed to her satisfaction. Making the bed up every morning only to unmake it that night constituted a total waste of time, in his often-voiced opinion. Once he had even found an article that declared beds should remain unmade during the day in order to discourage a proliferation of dust mites. The magazine had provided a most disturbing photograph of mites, magnified to display every detail of their nasty, leggy bodies. She still insisted on making the bed every day, but Al noticed that she changed the sheets twice a week after that.

Might as well confront the issue head-on. "What did I forget to do?"

She glanced at the screen, where an enthusiastic family from Kansas huddled in a knot to consult on the most frequent answer to the question, "Name something you might say to a cannibal to stop him from eating you." Her mouth tightened further.

"The upstairs bedrooms need to be dusted."

An obvious ploy to separate him from a television game show. "Why?"

"Because that's what I do on Fridays. I dust and run the vacuum upstairs."

"But no one's going to be using those rooms for at least a month." He turned back to the screen. "No one will ever know we skipped a week."

"I'll know." Out of the corner of his eye he saw her plant her good hand on her hip. The weight of the censure in her stare pressed on him. "Keeping a house clean is a continual process. One can't afford to become lax."

He might have voiced further arguments, but just then the family spokesperson answered. Apparently "I taste bad" was not the top answer, and the opposing family erupted into cheers. With an unconcealed sigh, Al picked up the remote control, punched the off button, and lowered the recliner's footrest.

"You're a slave driver." Though he infused enough teasing into his accusation that she wouldn't think he was truly complaining, an unexpected thought popped into his head. Returning to the office on Monday would be a relief. Computer work was far easier than being Millie's servant.

As he rose, the front doorbell chimed. Millie's eyes went wide, and her good hand flew to her hair. "I don't want anyone to see me looking like this."

"I'll get rid of them. Lulu took me unawares. I'm more prepared now."

He started for the front, but before he'd even crossed the bedroom floor a voice called from the hallway.

"Yoohoo! Are you decent?"

The stiffness melted from Millie's body. "It's only Violet." She raised her voice and shouted, "We're in the bedroom."

Moments later Violet swept into the room. She spared a quick nod at Al and then focused her attention on Millie. A frown creased her forehead below a tight row of curls the color of gun metal.

"Gracious, she was right. You look like a wraith."

Millie raised a hand self-consciously to her cheek. "Who's *she*?"

"That Thacker woman, of course." Violet crossed the bedroom, plucked at the skirt of Millie's housedress, and then inspected her hair. "She caught me in the yard before I saw her coming. Told me she'd been here and you look like death. Made it sound as if you're wasting away and barely able to hobble out of bed."

"Why would she say that?" Millie looked as dumbfounded as Al felt. "We had a nice visit this morning. I thought we might even become friends."

"Oh, you're her friend all right." Violet shook her head, distaste apparent on her face. "She wants to make sure you're taken care of in your hour of need. Told me she was about to make some calls to the church office to let them know you could use help with meals."

Al brightened. Though Millie was becoming acclimated to using one hand, she still relied on him to do the chopping and mixing required to cook. Under her eagle eye, of course. Even with her guidance, last night's cheeseburgers and salad left his taste buds feeling deprived. Eating a meal made by someone other than himself sounded like a far more enjoyable alternative.

Apparently Millie didn't think so. Horror crept over her features. "Oh, no! How long do you think I have?"

"I hurried over as soon as I could get away from her." Violet glanced at her watch. "I'd say the first will arrive within the hour."

Al shook his head. At times he suspected women had developed a form of communication not detectable by the male of the species. Some sort of gender-specific telepathy, maybe. Though he stood right here beside them, they both seemed to know what the other was thinking, while he hadn't a clue. "What do you mean by *the first*?"

They turned incredulous stares on him.

"The first of the casserole brigade, of course." Violet plucked at a limp lock of Millie's hair. "We might have time, if we hurry."

Millie nodded. "I'll plug in the hot rollers."

Al stepped out of the way when Violet headed for the closet. "I'll help you change. What about the straw skirt and pink blouse?"

The room became a bustle of female activity. Al stood in the doorway, watching. What was the casserole brigade, and why would Millie need to dress up for it? Shaking his head, he left the room unnoticed and headed for the hall closet, where Millie kept the cleaning supplies. If something called a "brigade" was on its way, perhaps being upstairs with a week's worth of dust wasn't a bad idea.

## Lulu Thacker's Parsnip Maple Cake

1 cup all-purpose flour
1 tsp. ground cinnamon
½ tsp. baking powder
½ tsp. baking soda
¼ tsp. salt
7 T. butter, room temperature, divided
²/₃ cup brown sugar
6 T. maple syrup, divided
½ tsp. imitation maple flavoring
1 egg
½ cup sour cream
¹/₃ cup dried cranberries
2 cups peeled and shredded parsnips (approx. 3-4 parsnips)
Approx. ½ cup chopped pecans (add an additional ¹/₃ cup
chopped pecans if you desire nuts in the cake)
½ cup confectioner's sugar

Preheat oven to 400 degrees. Grease and flour the bottom
and sides of an 8 x 8 glass cake pan.

Combine flour, cinnamon, baking powder, baking soda,
and salt in a bowl. Set aside.

Cream 4 tablespoons butter with brown sugar in a mixer
bowl. Turn on the mixer and add 4 tablespoons maple
syrup, 1 tablespoon at a time, and then the maple flavoring.
(If you use real maple syrup, you may eliminate the imitation maple flavoring.) Mix on medium speed until light and
creamy. Add the egg and continue beating until blended.

Add about half of the flour mixture, continuing to beat
until combined. When that is blended, add half the sour
cream and keep beating. Alternate the rest of the flour and

sour cream. Turn off the mixer and fold in the parsnips, cranberries, and (optional) ⅓ cup pecans.

Spread in the prepared pan. Bake for about 25 minutes or until a knife inserted in the center comes out clean. Run a knife around the inside edges and cool in pan.

*Maple Frosting:* In a small mixing bowl, beat 3 tablespoons butter and the confectioner's sugar until creamy. Continue to beat while drizzling in 2 to 3 tablespoons syrup until desired consistency. Spread over cooled cake and sprinkle ½ cup pecans over the top.

# Chapter Six

When Susan escorted Jeannie Quisenberry and her dog from the exam room to the reception desk, she cast a quick glance into the waiting rooms. Two cat owners sat in the area on the left, chatting quietly. The Wainright boys had taken possession of one corner of the Playful Pup room. A variety of action figures, Legos, and Matchbox cars surrounded them. At the moment they both knelt on the floor, using the seats of a couple of hard plastic chairs as desks. The younger's fingers tapped the screen of a tablet while the older sketched on a piece of paper. Though Susan might have suggested that they keep the place a bit tidier, at least they weren't disturbing anyone.

Jeannie extracted a credit card from her wallet and handed it to Alice. "When do I bring him back?"

"Today he got the last of his puppy shots. If he develops any problems, give us a call. Otherwise I'll see him again when he's a year old." Susan knelt to give the puppy a scratch behind the ears. "You'll be a big fella then, won't you?"

"And hopefully he'll be potty trained." Jeannie eyed her pet with a scowl that failed to hide her fondness. "Sorry about the mess in your exam room."

Susan chuckled and straightened. "Trust me, we're used to messes around here."

An indulgent smile came over the woman's face. "And how long until the wedding?"

"Twenty-eight days." Susan returned the smile, though with a touch of caution. After Justin's public proposal at the community Fourth of July softball game last summer, half the town felt like they'd played a part in the engagement. One reason why Susan was determined to keep the ceremony private. If she invited half the town, the other half would feel slighted. Best to invite no one at all rather than try to appease several hundred small-town egos.

"How exciting." Jeannie grinned. "The big day will be here before you know it."

As she turned to go, Susan's heart executed a crazy flutter. In twenty-eight days she would become Justin's wife. Susan Hinkle. Susan *Jeffries* Hinkle. *Doctor* Susan Hinkle. A notebook on her bedside table at home contained a few dozen practice signatures, but the one she'd scrawled most often, the one she preferred, was *Mrs. Justin Hinkle.*

With a farewell wave for Jeannie, Susan picked up the chart of the patient waiting in Exam Room One.

Alice rose from her chair. "Did she say Room Two needs cleaning?"

"If you don't mind." Susan couldn't stop a hint of apology from creeping into her tone. One of the most difficult things she'd had to learn about running a business was to delegate, especially the less pleasant tasks. She'd much rather do everything herself rather than have Alice or Millie feel that they were being taken advantage of. But she'd learned the hard way that one person could not run an animal clinic. Not efficiently, anyway.

"Of course not." Alice stood, and directed a stern comment toward her sons. "I'll be right back. Don't move."

The two spoke without looking up from their activities.

"'K, Mom."

"We won't."

When Alice disappeared through the door to the right of the

reception area, Susan spoke to the women in the Kuddly Kitties section. "Sorry for your wait. We'll be right with you."

Both ladies assured her they had not been waiting long and returned to their conversation. Turning to go, Susan hesitated a moment before approaching the boys in the other waiting room.

"You two are being really quiet. Thank you."

They twisted toward her and turned nearly identical gazes her way. The two could have been twins, though eleven-year-old Forest stood a few inches taller than Heath, the younger by a year. Both sported full heads of thick, unruly locks several shades darker than their mother's and a smattering of freckles across pert noses.

"Mom said if we bother you we're grounded from TV for a month," Forest informed her.

Heath added, "And we'll get a whupping too."

Forest regarded his brother. "Losing TV's worse 'cause it lasts longer."

"Yeah," his brother agreed. "'Sides, Mom's whuppings ain't bad unless she gets the big spoon."

Susan cleared her throat. She had never received a spanking as a child since Daddy did not believe in corporal punishment. But she'd been a calm, obedient girl. Poor Alice had her hands full raising five children on her own. What had happened to these boys' father? Alice had never said, and Susan didn't want to be a prying boss.

"What are you doing there, Heath?" She nodded toward the electronic tablet.

"Killing zombies." He glanced at the device and then threw his head back and let out an anguished cry. "Noooo! The zombies ate my brains while I wasn't looking."

Stomach slightly queasy, Susan turned to Forest. "And what are you drawing?" Hopefully something besides zombies.

"A horse." He held it aloft. "Only it looks more like a dog. I can't get the legs right."

Susan made a show of inspecting the drawing. "I think it looks pretty good."

"Nah, it's stupid." The boy's shoulders slumped. "And I don't got no more paper." He raised wide hazel eyes to hers. "Could I get some from the printer stand over there so's I can try again?"

If it would keep the child quiet, he could have a whole ream of printer paper. "Sure. Help yourself."

With a farewell nod, she headed toward the back, her next patient's chart in her hand. Justin was probably right. They weren't bad kids. They knew how to behave themselves when they wanted to.

※

The big tree in front of the animal clinic had lots of good climbing limbs once you shinnied up the lower part. Forest planted his foot and tested the branch he'd just reached, one arm around the trunk.

"I don't see her yet," Heath said from above.

Forest shielded his eyes with his free hand and looked down the length of the street. No sign of Fern. She'd been gone a long time.

"Maybe she got the job."

Confident in the sturdiness of the branch, he let go of the trunk and walked toe-to-toe outward until the surface narrowed and began to quiver beneath him. Then he dropped down to straddle the bark-covered limb.

Above him, Heath's stomach rumbled. "I wish she'd hurry. I'm hungry."

"You're always hungry." Though Forest's innards were starting to feel empty too. When Fern came to get them, they were going down to the Whistlestop to get a burger. They couldn't go to the drugstore for ice cream on account of Fern's getting fired from there, which was why she had to go to detention.

To take his mind off his hunger, he slipped his arms out of his backpack and swung it around. An unaccustomed heaviness dragged at his shoulders.

"Hey, look what I got." He unzipped the backpack and opened it to display the contents.

Heath leaned over his branch and peered down. "You got paper."

"Yeah, but look what kind." He pulled out a piece and held it up so his brother could read the printed section at the top.

"You got paper that has Goose Creek Animal Clinic on it." Heath shrugged. "So you gotta draw on the back where there ain't no writing."

"I'm not gonna draw on this paper." Forest returned the crisp white sheet to his backpack. "I'm gonna save it."

"For what?"

Forest shrugged. "Whatever."

He wasn't sure what use he'd find for a thick stack of the animal clinic's letterhead, but taking it had been too big a temptation. Especially when he had permission, so he wasn't even stealing. Someday he'd think of something to do with it.

"Hey!" Heath's excited shout reached him. "There she is."

Sure enough, Fern had just rounded the corner down the street. At the rate she was walking, he figured they had about four minutes before she arrived.

"We gotta be quick." He slung his backpack around, slipped his arms into the straps, and started the downward climb. "You still got the stuff, right?"

"Course I do."

Forest hung from the bottom branch by his arms and dropped the last six feet to the ground, Heath a few seconds behind him. They ran for the building, where Forest halted with his hand on the door handle.

"Okay," he instructed in a hoarse whisper, "I'll distract Mom while you hide the dog treats in the cat room and the catnip in the dog room. Be sure to hide everything good so the people won't see 'em."

Heath covered his mouth and giggled. "I hope there's some cats in there when the dogs go looking for those treats. Wish we could be there to see the ruckus."

"Are you kidding?" Forest asked. "Mom would know for sure who did it, and she'd kill us." He grinned at his brother. "But it sure is gonna be funny."

## Chapter Seven

Millie turned carefully in the car seat and accepted the hand Albert offered to help her stand. Her right wrist, protected by its brace and resting in a pretty, frilly sling Violet had made for her, felt much better this morning. Unless she moved it, of course.

"Are you sure you're okay?" Concern showed on Albert's face as he steadied her on the sidewalk in front of the Freckled Frog.

"I'm fine," she assured him for the fifth time in as many minutes. "I'm not planning to run a marathon. I'm only going to pop in and give Frieda an update, and then I'll join you over at the soda fountain."

He leaned into the car and retrieved the inflatable donut.

"Put that thing away," Millie whispered, glancing up and down the street to see if anyone had noticed. She loathed the necessity for the thing, and after Lulu's assumption yesterday, she wanted no one to mistake the reason for its use.

Albert's eyebrows arched. "You're going to stand the whole time?"

Catching sight of Frieda inside the display window, Millie snatched it from his hand and tossed it into the passenger seat. "Standing is more comfortable than sitting anyway."

With a shrug, Albert shut the car door. "Call me if you need help. I even turned on my phone." He patted the cell phone clipped to his belt and then headed across the railroad tracks that ran down the center of Main Street. His path intersected Fred Rightmier's approach, and Millie watched as the two shook hands and disappeared together inside Cardwell Drugstore. The jangle of the sleigh bells hanging inside the door reached her across the street just before they pulled it shut. On this sunny Saturday, no doubt the soda fountain would be full of Creekers.

She passed beneath the carved wooden arch that covered the entry and twisted the doorknob. Old and a bit creaky, the door proved stubborn and required an extra push, which Millie supplied without thinking. Ouch. The effort stressed sore muscles in her hindquarters, and she clamped her teeth against a swift intake of breath. The pain in her tailbone had receded to what she would describe as extreme soreness, but that was vastly preferable to the debilitating ache of the past two days.

Inside the store, Frieda called from the back room. "That you, Millie?"

"Yes."

"Be right out."

Millie pulled the door shut, gritting her teeth as she exerted enough effort to close it all the way across a splintered wooden threshold. Inside she paused a moment to take in the sight of Frieda's merchandise. She'd rearranged her potpourri of products a few months back into an artistic display of colors rather than grouping similar items together. A mistake, in Millie's closely held opinion. Though certainly decorative, the old arrangement of placing all the jewelry in one place and all the dishware in another seemed more orderly.

She passed a display shelf draped with red and silver, and ran a finger along the brim of a felt hat decorated with an impressive display of scarlet-colored feathers. Where would one wear such a thing? The Derby, perhaps?

Browns, reds, and yellows dominated the back corner, and Millie gravitated in that direction. She always enjoyed examining the hand-thrown pottery, though Frieda asked far too much for those pieces. No one who lived in Goose Creek ever bought them, but during the

Fall Festival, when the town overflowed with visitors, Frieda couldn't keep them on the shelves.

"Oh!" Millie halted her approach when she caught sight of a new piece. "Oh my."

Frieda appeared from the back room, a spray bottle in one hand and a rag in the other. "You found Chester, did you? I just got him last week. Interesting, don't you think?"

Resting on the center shelf of the pottery display was the ugliest bust of a head Millie had ever seen. The basic shape was of a jar, with a narrow opening at the top glazed to resemble a hat such as an organ grinder's monkey might wear. A huge mouth filled with uneven, yellowish teeth protruded between cracked brown lips. A large, blobby nose took up half the face, and misshapen flaps on each side served as ears. But what drew her attention were the huge round eyeballs resting inside bulging lids beneath lumps of clay painted to look like hairy eyebrows. A shudder rippled across her shoulders. Those eyeballs looked like they'd caught sight of her and were preparing to follow her home.

"*Interesting* is not how I'd describe it." Millie turned away from the hideous statue and suppressed an urge to rub the back of her head, positive his stare was still fixed on her. "Why did you take it in on consignment? Surely you don't think anyone will buy it."

Frieda cocked her head and examined the ghastly thing. "Oh, I don't know. He kind of grows on you after a while. I named him Chester because his ears remind me of a guy I dated in high school." She shook her head. "Poor boy. I heard he had them docked a few years later."

"What's the price on, uh, Chester?"

"Three hundred dollars. He's handmade, after all."

Millie arched an eyebrow. Anyone who would pay three hundred dollars for that repulsive effigy, even if it was handmade, needed to have their own head examined.

Frieda stepped behind the sales counter and began scooting things out of the way. "I was so busy yesterday I didn't get a chance to make anything, but I'll bring over a chicken and rice casserole tomorrow after church."

Millie rushed to answer. "Oh, please don't go to any trouble. I had almost a dozen visitors yesterday, so we have plenty of food to see us through this minor setback."

In fact, the casserole brigade had outperformed any previous undertaking in recent memory. Their refrigerator and freezer were crammed with such a variety of dishes that Albert had threatened to throw the late arrivals in the trash bin. Among the gifts from the well-wishers were a green bean casserole, hamburger-potato casserole, tuna casserole, ham and noodle casserole, turkey tetrazzini, enchilada casserole, a lasagna, and no less than three different versions of broccoli casserole. Not to mention a pot of chicken soup, six dozen cookies, a chocolate pie, and of course Lulu's parsnip cake.

At the look of slight offense on Frieda's face, Millie added, "Of course your chicken and rice is my favorite, but I know it takes a lot of effort, and I'll be fine in a day or two. I'm already much better."

That seemed to appease her. "So you're going to help Lulu Thacker with this historical society stuff?" Millie nodded, and Frieda went on. "I'm relieved to hear it. The celebration committee needs that money, and she'll bungle it for sure."

Though Millie understood the concern, having observed Lulu's brash manner more than once, she felt the need to speak a word in her defense. Frieda was known to be harsh, and her gossip sometimes a bit mean-spirited.

"I'm sure she could do a fine job on her own," she said, "but since I've already done a lot of the legwork we decided it only made sense to work together."

"Well, I don't envy you. That woman's got some weird ways about her. And her husband too."

Not a statement Millie could dispute, which was why she'd

ventured out this morning without Lulu in tow. Best to handle the initial contacts with more tact than Lulu possessed.

She changed the subject. "Since I missed the last meeting, I wanted to stop by and make sure you understand that this Main Street Program isn't something Lulu and I can do on our own. If we're going to be approved by the state to participate in the program, we'll need the support of the city council and the majority of the town's business owners. We're meeting with the mayor Monday morning, but I wanted to talk to you first."

Frieda paused in the act of clearing the counter, a frown on her face. "What kind of support?"

"The purpose of the program—wait a minute." She reached into her purse and pulled out the folded paper she'd printed from the program's website last night. "*To support economic development through historical preservation. The program's efforts center on revitalizing the city's downtown area.*"

Frieda brightened. "I like that. Revitalization is what this town needs. That'll be good for business."

Millie knew she would approve of that aspect. But the next? "There may be some things that building owners need to change, though. That's the *historical preservation* part."

"You mean like fixing up that sagging porch awning over Wade's used bookstore, or the crumbling bricks on the Hockensmiths' harness shop?"

"Yes. It might cost some money." Frieda's scowl returned, and Millie hurried on before she could interrupt. "But part of the benefit of being in the program is the Kentucky Heritage Council. They have all kinds of ways to help. They can walk us through the tax credit process, and other programs too. They even have architects who are experts on historical stuff and will draw up blueprints for free."

"Well." Frieda cocked her head to consider. "All that sounds fine, but it's gonna take some fast talking to convince Brett Hockensmith to part with a penny." She lowered her voice and leaned across the counter. "I told them when they opened that place there wasn't enough horse business in this area to keep a tack store afloat, but would they listen?"

"That's where I think you can help." Millie came to the point of this morning's visit. "You're a well-respected business owner. If anyone can convince them that this is a good idea, it's you."

A small smile curved Frieda's thin lips. "I do have a way with people."

Though Frieda's *way with people* bordered on pushy, at least she had the connections with the downtown community that Lulu and Millie did not. "But we have to move fast. Lulu and I are already working on the application, but it usually takes months, and the approval process can be months longer. We've got to sell Goose Creek on the program, and then we need to convince the Heritage Council to accelerate our application. Otherwise we won't have a chance at that private grant money."

Millie had saved that last bit for impact. Since the grant money would provide the funds for Frieda's pet project, the reminder should provide the final nudge she needed.

"Count me in," Frieda announced. "Tell me what we want them to agree to, and I'll make sure they do."

Millie breathed a relieved sigh. The first obstacle overcome.

Frieda sprayed the glass-covered counter and then applied her cleaning rag with energy. The air filled with a pleasant lemon scent.

"Mmm, that smells good." Millie glanced at the small label, on which was handwritten in neat print, *Lemon Cleaning Spray.* "What is it?"

"Oh, some sort of natural cleaning solution. Got it from Tuesday." She cast a scowl toward the storefront and the day spa on the other side of the railroad tracks. "There's another weird one, but she does have some good ideas."

"I like her." Millie readily defended the flighty massage therapist.

"Well," Frieda said grudgingly, "she has dressed up the downtown area a bit with her work on that day spa of hers. Though I wish she'd consulted me before painting her storefront purple. After all, I have to look out my front window at it every day." She gave the counter-top a final swipe as Millie turned to leave. "One good thing, anyway. I won't have to make any expensive changes to my shop. I keep the outside neat as a pin."

Millie thought it best not to comment as she jerked the sticking door open and stepped over the uneven threshold.

Outside, she paused and tilted her face toward the sun. April still had two days left, but the air held the May-like scent of sweet grasses and freshly plowed soil. The soybeans in Barry Yates's front field had already begun to poke tender green shoots up through the ground. Millie battled a stab of frustration. If she hadn't injured her wrist, this would have been the perfect weekend to set impatiens in the front flower boxes.

She headed across the street, stepping carefully over the slightly protruding rails on the crosswalk. As she reached the opposite side, a car pulled into one of the diagonal parking places to her right. Agnes Peach emerged and called a greeting.

"Good to see you out and about. Feeling better this morning, are you?"

"Much better, thank you."

"I'm going to pop in here and pick up some nail polish." She stepped up onto the curb and headed for Tuesday's Day Spa. Through the front window of the drugstore, Millie glimpsed several people seated at the soda fountain counter. The Saturday morning Creek-ers were well represented today, so Albert would be fine on his own for a while. In fact, it would be good for him to spend time with his friends without her. After two days of helping around the house, he was beginning to get grouchy.

She followed Agnes through the bright purple door, noting how easily it swung outward on well-oiled hinges. Justin had done a beauti-ful job remodeling this building, despite the unfortunate color choice.

After the colorful hodgepodge of the Freckled Frog, stepping into the Day Spa felt like sipping a cool glass of lemonade on a warm summer afternoon. The subtle scent of lavender wafting from a flickering candle somehow blended with the quiet lilt of a strumming guitar to create an atmosphere of instant relaxation. In contrast to the dramatic purple of the spa's exterior, faint lilac walls and soft gray trim created a quiet, dreamy atmosphere. Millie pulled the door shut behind her, tension seeping from her muscles.

Tuesday's voice came from behind the walled-off partition that formed a private area where she performed massages. "Be with y'all in just a minute. Help yourself to tea while you wait."

"No rush," Millie called, and then joined Agnes at a table set along the right-hand wall, where a ceramic coffee urn containing hot water rested beside a display of herbal teas.

Agnes tore open a packet and dropped a tea bag into a cup. "I hope my casserole was edible. I used a different recipe this time."

While Millie selected a mug from the stand, her mind filtered through the various offerings that filled her refrigerator. Had Agnes brought the enchiladas or the tetrazzini? Best to keep her reply generic.

She offered a smile and picked up a packet of peppermint tea. "We had Cindie's beef and noodles last night, but Albert is looking forward to trying yours tonight. I'm sure it will be delicious."

"Well, let me know."

After dunking her bag only a few times, Agnes tossed it into the trash and took her mug to a rack of all-natural nail polish on the opposite wall. Millie glanced at the bin. What a waste. After such a brief dousing, there was plenty of flavor still in that tea bag. She deliberately let hers steep until the scent of peppermint became robust enough to almost overpower the lavender candle. She hesitated over the sugar bowl. At home she would have added an artificial sweetener, but Tuesday was an outspoken naturalist and did not offer an alternative to sugar. Well, peppermint provided a flavor to be enjoyed on its own, even without the added sweetness.

Turning, she glanced toward the pedicure chair in the corner and was half-tempted to ask if Tuesday had time to fit her in. Bright sunshine and warming days heralded the onset of sandal season, which one couldn't enter with winter-dull toenails.

No, no pedicure today with Albert acting as chauffeur. He would chafe at having to wait for her. Besides, sitting in a chair that long without the donut would be agonizing.

She eyed the two chairs arranged on this side of the massage partition, an inviting assortment of magazines on the table between them. Instead she crossed to a display counter near the nail polish rack. Tuesday made and sold scented soy candles in a variety of colors, shapes, and scents.

A bottle of pink polish in her hand, Agnes joined her in front of the counter. "I know everyone says soy is better, but I'm not convinced there's really that much of a difference."

"Oh, honey, there's a huge difference." Tuesday emerged from the massage room, a length of floral print chiffon floating behind her. She approached and picked up a sea green pillar. "Soy burns longer and cleaner, and besides, it's vegetable-based. You don't get any of the nastiness of paraffin candles, like soot. You know the stuff that collects in your furniture and turns your ceiling black? Paraffin is a petroleum by-product." Eyes wide, she leaned forward to emphasize her point. "Why, you might as well back a diesel truck up to your front door and fill your house with exhaust."

Judging by the faintly horrified expression on Agnes's face, she must have owned a few paraffin candles.

Millie gestured toward a row of spray bottles on a nearby counter that were new since her last visit to the Day Spa. "Frieda was using this when I was over at her shop. When did you start selling cleaning products?"

Beaming, Tuesday replaced the candle and picked up a bottle. "Just this week. I've been making this stuff for years, so I decided I might as well sell it."

Impressed, Millie glanced around the room. Besides being a naturalist, Tuesday was something of an entrepreneur. Either that, or the massage and pedicure business wasn't brisk enough to support her, and the addition of her homemade products was an attempt to supplement her income.

"I'll try one," Millie said, pushing aside the guilty thought of the many bottles of spray cleanser beneath the kitchen sink at home.

"Thanks, hon." Clearly pleased, Tuesday picked up a bottle and crossed to a small desk where she kept a calculator and a cash box.

Cheryl Lawson emerged from the massage room, her hair rumpled and her eyelids drooping. Her purse dangled from her fingers. "Ahhh." Her lips curved into a languid smile. "That was wonderful."

Grinning, Tuesday filled a paper cup from a water cooler in the corner and handed it to Cheryl. "Be sure to drink plenty of water today."

"I will." Cheryl pulled a check out of her purse and handed it to Tuesday, and then caught sight of Millie. Concern creased her forehead. "I heard about your accident. How are you feeling?"

Forcing a smile, Millie said, "It wasn't an accident, just a silly little mishap. I'm fine." For a quick change of subject, she addressed Tuesday. "In fact, I'm here on official business. I'll be working with Lulu to put together our Main Street application, and we need to make sure we have the support of the town's business owners."

Tuesday brightened. "You bet I'll support you. I'm all for free money wherever we can find it."

Agnes advanced to Millie's side. "What's this about free money?"

Millie explained the program briefly, encouraged by Tuesday's vigorous nods.

"That *sounds* good," Cheryl said, her tone flooded with doubt. "All except the part where Lulu Thacker is in charge. She's a newcomer to the Creek. Shouldn't we have one of our own leading the effort?"

A pair of bright spots appeared high on Tuesday's cheeks. She, too, was relatively new to Goose Creek, and until she'd proven herself by investing a significant amount of money in the town's economy with her renovations for her business, had suffered the scorn of the long-time residents. Including, to Millie's recollection, Cheryl herself.

Before the kindhearted massage therapist could make an ill-conceived reply, Millie leaped to Lulu's defense. "The position involves a lot of work, and not many people would be willing to make the commitment."

Agnes appeared thoughtful, but Cheryl crossed her arms, her demeanor stubborn.

"Besides," Millie rushed on, "Lulu has already gotten involved in the town's affairs. She volunteered for the celebration committee, and…" She cast around for a compliment that would speak well of her new friend's commitment. "And she hasn't missed a single meeting."

"That's right, she hasn't." Tuesday edged closer to Millie in what might have been an unconscious show of solidarity.

"But she doesn't know us," Cheryl insisted. "And we don't know her."

"That's where I come in. She recognizes that an in-depth knowl-edge of Goose Creek's history is necessary, so she asked me to help." Not exactly the truth, but Millie saw no reason to admit that Lulu was afraid she'd offend Goose Creek business owners with her brash manner.

"With Millie's help she'll do just fine." Tuesday put an arm around Millie's shoulders and squeezed, a gesture that abused her sore muscles to the point that she had to force herself not to grimace. "And maybe you ought to try to get to know her. She's a real nice lady."

"Well." Cheryl shouldered her purse strap. "I guess the decision's been made, so it's too late to argue about. Let's just hope she can get us some of that grant money."

She left the building, and while Tuesday calculated Agnes's pur-chases—nail polish and a vanilla-scented soy candle—Millie watched through the front window as Cheryl crossed the street. She disap-peared inside the Freckled Frog, and Millie relaxed. Frieda would not tolerate any hint of negativity circulating about this project. She would set Cheryl straight.

❄

Susan hefted a cardboard box out of her car, propped it on the bumper, and slammed the trunk. Though her burden was not large, the textbooks inside gave it enough weight to require a bit of exertion, and she grunted as she lifted it off the bumper.

Justin, walking backward up the porch steps of their new home carrying one end of a dresser, called to her. "Leave that, Suz. I'll get it in a minute." His words were clipped short as he strained under a far greater weight than this little box. At the other end of the dresser, Junior Watson lifted his half with no visible effort.

"I've got it," she called back. Under no circumstances would she stand by like a helpless female and let the guys do all the heavy lifting.

She carried her burden up the three concrete steps, panting only a little. At her approach, Charlie appeared from inside the house and took the box from her hands. With a grin, he lifted it up and balanced it on one shoulder as if it contained nothing heavier than a pillow.

"Show-off." She smiled so he'd know she was joking. He had been working for Justin for only a month or so, and she didn't know him well.

He flashed a good-natured grin in return. "Where's this one go?"

"In my office."

She pointed down the hallway to the small bedroom they had designated as hers. Since Justin would be running his handyman business from here, he would set up his office in the larger one.

Alone in the main room, she gazed around and filled the empty space mentally with the furniture they had picked out. The sofa would go there against the far wall and would face two chairs angled to form a cozy conversation niche around the fireplace. No coffee table, lest the small area feel cluttered, but a pair of adorable occasional tables would add to the comfortable atmosphere she hoped to create. She could hardly wait for them to be delivered so she could see them in place.

Footsteps on the stairs drew her attention, and she turned to see her fiancé descending from the loft they had decided would be their bedroom. Warmth filled her at the sight of him, his hair in disarray and dark curls dampened by a sheen of sweat on his forehead. *Mr. and Mrs. Justin Hinkle.*

"That's the last of it," he said as he reached the floor. "Can't thank you enough for the use of the truck and your strong back, Junior."

"Ain't no problem." The big man pulled a bandanna out of the chest pocket of his denim overalls and swiped it across the back of his neck. "I know you'uns would do the same if'n I needed the help."

"You know it." Justin clapped his shoulder. "Just say the word."

Puzzlement crept over Junior's face. "Uh…please?"

Susan hid a smile. "What he means is all you have to do is ask and we'll be glad to return the favor."

Junior's expression cleared. "Okay."

Charlie returned. "Is that all there is?"

Since she rented a furnished apartment and Justin had sold many of the bits and pieces he'd picked up at garage sales when he moved in with the Richardsons last year, the sum of their possessions had fit in a single truckload.

"That's it. Thanks for your help, Charlie. See you Monday. I'll pick you up at seven."

"You bet, Boss."

The two men departed, leaving Susan and Justin alone in their new home.

He scrunched his features. "I wish he wouldn't call me Boss. It sounds so official."

She laughed and stepped closer, drawn like metal to a magnet. "That's the price of success." A rogue curl stuck out on one side, and she smoothed it into place over his ear. "I felt the same the first time someone called me Dr. Jeffries. Like I was pretending to be a grown-up."

Hooking an arm around her waist, he drew her to him. "How are you going to feel when they call you Dr. Hinkle?"

A delicious thrill shot through her. "I'll probably grin like an idiot."

He lowered his head and their lips met, sending a multitude of shivers coursing through her. The kiss ended too soon, her lips reluctant to release his. She stepped prudently away, aware that the rigid self-control she had exercised all her life in any endeavor she undertook was rendered feeble and fragile in close proximity to the man she loved. An equal passion shone in the eyes that bore into hers, and she cleared her throat. Time for a little ice water.

"Your Aunt Lorna called today."

Rolling his eyes, he heaved a sigh. "Again?"

"Twice, actually." The second time, Susan had felt obligated to take the call. "She's upset about the flowers."

"What flowers? I thought we decided not to have flowers."

"Exactly." The conversation had lasted far longer than Susan's patience, and Mrs. Ryan informed her in no uncertain terms that she and her cat did not appreciate being kept waiting in a cold exam room. "She insists that it's bad luck for a bride to not carry a bouquet, and I'm dooming our marriage before it even begins."

Justin made a rude sound with his lips. "I hope you told her to mind her own business."

"Of course not, but I didn't give in either." She allowed a touch of doubt to creep into her voice. "She's your great-aunt, Justin. I don't have a relationship with any of my relatives, so I don't want to alienate her. Maybe I should carry a few daisies or something, just to make her happy."

He took her hand and led her to the wall where the sofa would go, and they sank to the floor to sit side by side.

"Aunt Lorna's a tough old bird and a lot harder to offend than you think. If you give in on the flowers, she'll see that as an open door. She'll elbow her way into every detail, and before you know it, we'll be getting married at St. Paul's Cathedral."

"Don't be silly. She can't be that bad." She leaned sideways to nudge his shoulder with hers. "When was the last time you saw her, anyway?" Susan decided to skip relating the part of the conversation where Aunt Lorna lamented the fact that the family had abandoned her and left a helpless old woman to die a lonely death in the frozen north.

"Let's see. It's been…" He leaned his head against the wall, eyes closed as he considered. "Seven years? She came down when my brother graduated from college. No, wait." He opened his eyes, and Susan detected a glint of sadness in them. "It was mom's funeral. Kevin and I took her ashes up to Boston and stayed with Aunt Lorna. So it's been five years."

Susan slipped her hand into his and intertwined their fingers. She'd lost her mother when she was young, but at least she still had Daddy. Justin's father died of a heart attack when he was in high school, so the loss of his mother left him with no parents. His brother, Kevin, lived in Texas, and his grandparents were gone as well. So really, Aunt Lorna was the only family he had left besides a distant cousin.

"I'm looking forward to meeting her and your cousin."

"Ross?" A smile replaced the sad expression. "I'm kind of surprised he's coming. It's not like we were close or anything. We're like third cousins, or maybe second cousins once removed or something like that. I haven't seen him since I was a kid."

"See?" Susan squeezed his hand. "Aunt Lorna had a good idea inviting him. It'll be like a mini family reunion."

A scowl gathered on his brow. "Well, she could have asked before inviting him. We told her she was the only family being included."

"Daddy did the same thing when he invited Uncle Mark without asking." Now it was Susan's turn to scowl. Mark wasn't really even her uncle. He'd been Daddy's college roommate. The only reason he was coming at all was because he planned to make a vacation out of the trip and go to the horse races at Churchill Downs.

"Hey, if your dad wants to include his buddy, that's okay with me." Justin shrugged.

She indulged in a smile and leaned her head sideways to rest on his shoulder. Justin was quick to defend anything Daddy did, an undisguised attempt to curry favor with the man who had staunchly disapproved of their relationship at first. What a relief that the two men in her life had made peace. At times she even suspected they were starting to like each other.

"So you think definitely no on the flowers?" she asked.

"Suz, do what *you* want to do. If you want to hold flowers when we get married, great. If you want me to wear a flower in my lapel, I will." A low chuckle rumbled in his chest. "Heck, I'll even put a rose behind each ear and hold one in my teeth if you want. But don't do it because of Aunt Lorna."

"I'd kind of like to see you with a rose behind each ear."

Her giggle faded into a comfortable silence.

He tilted his head to rest his cheek against her hair. "It's kind of sad, really. Neither of us has many relatives."

"I know. I'm an only child, Daddy and my mother were both only children...I don't think my grandfather had any siblings either. I guess I come from a long line of single-kid families."

Justin executed a deft twisting maneuver that ended with Susan in his lap, her face inches from his. "How about we see what we can do about breaking that trend?"

His mouth covered hers, and she returned his kiss with enthusiasm. The next twenty-eight days would be the longest of her life.

# Tuesday's Natural All-Purpose Cleanser

3 cups water
⅓ cup Castile soap
2 T. white vinegar
15 drops essential oil, such as lemon or peppermint

Combine all ingredients in a spray bottle. Use this cleanser as a natural alternative in the kitchen, bathroom, or anywhere you would use traditional spray cleanser.

Castile soap is a natural product made from vegetable oil instead of animal fat, as many traditional cleansers are. Thus, this cleanser is vegan-friendly.

# Chapter Eight

At ten o'clock sharp on Monday morning, Millie and Lulu stepped out of the elevator on the second floor of city hall. Millie had selected a dignified navy-blue sling from the half-dozen Violet had made for her. Lulu carried an ancient briefcase, its leather straps stretched and creased. Franklin's first attaché case after he left college, she'd told Millie earlier.

They were greeted by Sally Bright, the mayor's secretary.

Sally's pleasant expression faded, replaced by concern as her gaze rested on Millie's sling. "I didn't get a chance to speak with you after church yesterday. How are you feeling?"

The question was uttered in the pitying tone that was starting to get on Millie's nerves. In fact, the onslaught of questioners she'd faced yesterday at the close of the service had forced her to desert her normal practice of gathering on the front sidewalk for a half hour or so of amiable chitchat. She'd escaped as quickly as possible to avoid the plethora of sympathetic well-wishes.

She kept her face pleasant. "I'm fine, thank you."

Lulu, who was apparently oblivious to the fact that Millie preferred to avoid discussions of the unfortunate incident, blew a raspberry. "Don't let her fool you." Her brash voice filled the room as if she were shouting through a megaphone. "She's still mighty tender in the tush area, if you know what I mean."

Heat leaped into Millie's face. "Is Jerry ready for us?" she asked quickly to divert the conversation.

Sally nodded. "Go on in. He's expecting you." Millie headed for the door when Sally added, "Frieda's been in there for ten minutes already."

That drew Millie up short. Frieda had not been included in the meeting. She exchanged a glance with Lulu, who shrugged her boney shoulders.

Millie rapped a knuckle on the heavy wooden door before opening it. Frieda, seated in one of the three guest chairs on this side of the mayor's wide oak desk, turned at their entrance. Was her expression a bit shamefaced? Millie couldn't tell because she looked away so quickly.

Mayor Jerry Selbo rose from his high-backed chair behind the desk. "Come on in, ladies. Have a seat."

He gestured toward the two empty chairs. One matched the one Frieda had selected, the seat constructed of padded vinyl. The second, obviously added for their benefit before their arrival, was of polished hardwood.

Lulu stomped forwarded with her long-legged stride and claimed the wooden chair. "You sit there," she told Millie, pointing at the other. "It'll be softer on your backside."

Face flaming, Millie lowered herself into the vinyl chair. She really must ask Lulu not to mention her rear end in public.

Jerry, at least, possessed enough courtesy to withhold comment, and waited until they were all settled before returning to his chair.

"Frieda was just explaining the Main Street Program." He rested his clasped hands on the blotter in front of him. "It certainly sounds like something the town should pursue."

Millie turned her head to give Frieda an undisguised look of inquiry.

The owner of the Freckled Frog failed to meet her eye. "You told me you were meeting with the mayor this morning, so I thought I'd stop in before I open my shop and assure him of my support, both as a business owner and as the chair of the celebration committee."

"Good thinking." Lulu gave a nod.

Studying Frieda through narrowed eyes, Millie decided there was more to this visit than she was letting on. The woman fiddled with the straps of the handbag resting in her lap, a nervous gesture that Millie had never seen the outspoken shop owner exhibit.

Turning her attention to Jerry, she smiled. "Since you've already been brought up-to-date on the purpose of the program, we won't need to explain it."

"But here's some stuff for you to look at." Lulu whipped a stack of papers from her briefcase and plopped them on the desk. "We got it off the website."

"Have you begun putting the application together yet?" Frieda asked.

"You betcha." Lulu patted the case. "We're heading over to Frankfort when we leave here so we can take a gander at other towns' applications."

"The Kentucky Heritage Council has them all on file," Millie added.

"We're nailing this thing down," Lulu said with confidence. "Gonna have everything ready to go before the next city council meeting." She looked at the mayor. "That way you can approve it quick-like, and we can get it filed. Soon as that's done, I'll start putting together a bid for some of that grant money." A satisfied smile on her wide lips, she sat back in her chair.

The mayor looked up from his perusal of the documents, eyebrows arched high. "You're planning on putting together the bid for the grant?" He slid a confused glance toward Frieda. "But I thought the Main Street Manager would undertake that task."

An uncomfortable tickle erupted in Millie's stomach. With a sideways look at Frieda, she said, "Lulu *is* the Main Street Manager. Or at least, she will be when our application is approved."

Now Frieda fidgeted openly. "Well, that's something I'm planning to bring up next Thursday at our meeting. The way I understood it, the city council is supposed to select the Main Street Manager."

"We talked about that," Lulu said, her confusion apparent. "You said you didn't want the job, and so did everybody else. I said I'd like to do it, and you said okay."

Frieda flashed an apologetic glance at Lulu before returning to her examination of her purse. "Perhaps we weren't clear in our expectations of the role we assigned to you. What we needed was someone who would pull together our application. We didn't necessarily mean that person would also manage the town's Main Street Program. After all, there might be someone else who would also be interested."

The situation bloomed with full clarity in Millie's mind. Cheryl Lawson, who'd made no secret of her disapproval of Lulu, had left the Day Spa on Saturday, marched directly across the street to the Freckled Frog, and poisoned Frieda against her.

Lulu shook her head. "That's not what you said on Thursday. You said—"

Frieda held up a hand. "I'm aware of Thursday's discussion. I was there. What I'm saying now is perhaps we need to rethink the decision. Perhaps we should consider someone"—she cleared her throat—"more suitable to the management job."

The itch erupted into simmering anger. Millie straightened her spine, barely noticing the discomfort that movement caused, and twisted to face Frieda directly. "More suitable in what way?"

At least this time Frieda met her eye. "Experience. Relationships with the town's business owners. An in-depth knowledge of Goose Creek's history."

Why, she was parroting Millie's own words to Cheryl and using them against her!

In a tone so meek Millie almost didn't recognize the speaker, Lulu said, "That's a good point."

Millie whirled on her—another ill-advised movement—and

found Lulu staring dejectedly at her hands, folded and resting in her lap. Her thin shoulders drooped. A protective wave, so fierce it surprised Millie, welled up inside her.

Before she could come up with a suitable reply, Jerry gave a little cough. They directed their attention to him.

"Seems to me that part of the report to the council should be a recommendation for the person who will become the Main Street Manager. I'll let you ladies work out that recommendation among you."

He placed his palms on the desk and pushed himself to a standing position, a clear dismissal. Teeth clamped together, and not just against the pain of rising, Millie followed suit. Jerry came around the desk and, with a hand resting lightly on Frieda's back, led them to the door.

"I understand you're working under time constraints, so if we need to call a special council session to approve your application, we will." He shook their hands in turn. "I look forward to reading your report."

When they all stood beside Sally's desk, the mayor's door closed with a soft *snick* behind them.

Millie rounded on Frieda. "That was inexcusable."

The shop owner had the grace to look embarrassed. But then she raised her chin and spoke in a determined manner. "The more I thought about it, I realized the Main Street Program isn't a matter for the celebration committee alone. We hope to get some of the grant money, of course, but it's a commitment that will last long after Goose Creek's century-and-a-half anniversary. Our committee overstepped our authority by what amounts to hiring a city employee."

"A *volunteer.*"

She waved a hand. "Whatever. The role of the Main Street Manager is an issue that needs wider input."

Millie planted her feet. "Input from who? Your friend Cheryl, perhaps?"

Frieda's gaze dropped, and Millie had the satisfaction of seeing a flush rise on her cheeks. Then she stepped around Millie and approached Lulu.

"Please don't take this personally." She clasped Lulu's hand in both of hers. "I can't tell you how much I appreciate your spearheading the application process. And you never know. Maybe it will be decided that you *are* the best candidate for the Main Street Manager after all."

If she weren't trying so hard to control her temper, Millie would have given a derisive laugh. She didn't believe Frieda's sincerity for a second. She and Cheryl were longtime friends, and Lulu an awkward outsider. No, they would come up with someone else to recommend for the job.

Lulu appeared to take the comment at face value. "Thank you for saying that."

Without another glance at Millie, Frieda left the room. Bypassing the elevator, she disappeared behind the heavy doors leading to the stairway.

Seated at her desk, Sally watched her go and then turned toward them, one eyebrow cocked. "Sounds like that was an interesting meeting."

A clear bid for information, which Millie was not prepared to supply. No doubt the mayor would fill her in after they'd gone.

"Come on, Lulu." She looped her good arm through Lulu's gangly one and steered her toward the elevator. "We'll talk about this on the way to Frankfort."

Uncharacteristically subdued, Lulu allowed Millie to lead her away.

# Chapter Nine

The first Saturday in May dawned bright and clear, exactly the kind of day a Kentuckian would want for Derby Day. Though not a racing enthusiast herself, Millie had decided several months ago to gather a few friends for a traditional Derby party. Her unfortunate incident notwithstanding, she'd been anticipating the opportunity to host her first official party in their new home since the house was beginning to resemble the grand place she envisioned it would one day be. Though her wrist had become a fascinating display of purple and yellow hues, in the past week she'd managed to become quite adept at one-handed activities and was able to mostly ignore the nighttime throbbing that resulted from overuse.

At least now she was able to sit in a proper chair and, as long as she positioned herself carefully, experienced only mild discomfort in her nether region.

Violet arrived for the party at one o'clock bearing her contributions to the menu.

"Country ham and beaten biscuits," she announced as she set a loaded tray of the traditional Derby fare on the dining room table. "My electric knife conked out on me, so I've taken a beating myself, slicing all that ham by hand."

"I'm sure everyone will appreciate your efforts." Millie stepped back and inspected her friend's hat. "Goodness, that's…quite colorful."

"Isn't it?" Violet preened and raised a hand to brush one of the orange feathers arranged on the wide, floppy rim. "Amazing what you can do with a trip to the dollar store and a hot glue gun."

Millie felt it best to confine her comments to a nod and an agreeable, "Amazing."

She'd selected a simple cloche hat with a satin band and a subdued bow. Gazing at Violet's elaborate creation, she felt satisfied with her choice.

"Did you see the price of the blue one down at the Frog?" Violet shook her head, *tsk*ing. "Three hundred dollars for a felt hat and a bit of fancy frippery. Safe to say she'll have that one in the store for a while."

At the mention of the Freckled Frog, Millie's lips tightened of their own accord, and she busied herself adjusting the placement of the linen napkins beside the stack of china plates. "Can't say I have."

Violet planted her hands on her hips. "I wish you two would get over this silly disagreement."

"It isn't silly." Millie battled a flash of resentment. Violet, her dearest friend for more than thirty years, had refused to side with her over the issue of the Main Street Manager. "I can't abide the unfairness of her expecting Lulu to do all the work involved in getting the program approved and then hand it over to someone else to run."

A sulky expression settled on Violet's face. "All I ever hear from you is Lulu this and Lulu that. It almost sounds like you're fond of her, when I know you think she's as nutty as a fruitcake, like the rest of us do."

*The rest of us.* Millie delayed replying by rearranging one of the roses in the huge crystal vase in the center of the table. She'd never intended for a line to be drawn and sides taken. Now that they had, it stung to find herself in opposition to her best friend.

And though Lulu was not nutty, she definitely was annoying. Over the past week Millie had been tied to her side as they traveled all across

Kentucky, visiting towns that had adopted the Main Street Program. They'd met with five different Main Street Managers, and more than once she'd found herself blushing at her new friend's thoughtless comments. She'd offended the manager of Carrollton with a disparaging word about their sidewalk repairs, and Millie would never dare to show her face in Covington again after the derogatory remarks about the statues along their Riverwalk.

Still, friendship had blossomed during those long drives in Lulu's car. Barriers had fallen, and confidences were shared. What had begun in Millie as compassion for an awkward woman who'd asked for her help had grown into genuine affection. Lulu meant well, she really did. Millie had discovered that her heart was as big as her mouth, and not nearly as bumbling.

The flower display finally arranged to her satisfaction, Millie turned to face Violet. "I am fond of her. It's true she's a bit overbearing, but she means well."

Violet's flaring nostrils spoke her disagreement louder than words. Had the doorbell not rung at that moment, they might have had words. Instead, Millie bustled from the room, feeling guilty to be relieved to escape.

The door opened as she entered the hall.

"Happy Derby Day!" Justin shouted as he stepped aside to allow Susan to enter ahead of him.

"And to you." Millie banished the lingering unpleasantness and stepped forward to kiss his cheek. "I miss you. The house feels empty without you."

In the week since Justin moved out, Millie had been surprised to find herself struggling with some of the same empty-nest emotions she'd experienced when Alison married and moved to Italy. The sound of Albert's loafers on the floor didn't compare to the stomp of Justin's work boots tromping up the stairs at the end of a long day.

"I'm so glad you were able to come." Millie turned to welcome her employer with a hug, careful not to disturb the foil-covered pie pan she carried. "You look lovely, dear. That fascinator is very attractive on you."

Susan preened, an unusual sight for the serious young woman. "I had so much fun picking it out." She tilted her head to show off the lace and ribbon design clipped in her hair. "I've never shopped for a Derby hat before."

"That one's a good choice." She eyed the pie. "And what did you bring to share with us?"

A proud smile appeared as Susan extended her offering. "Derby Pie, made in my own kitchen. Even if I don't actually live there yet." The smile dimmed. "It probably isn't very good. It still looked a little jiggly when the recipe said to take it out of the oven, so I left it in. The crust got kind of black."

"I'm sure it will be delicious," Millie said as the doorbell chimed again.

Justin, who was closest, opened it to reveal Tuesday Love on the porch, her features nearly obscured by a floppy straw hat with a garden's worth of purple flowers on the brim. "I hope I'm not late," she said as she entered. "I got halfway here and realized I'd forgotten my shoes."

She extended a foot to display a sandal with the tallest spiked heels Millie had ever seen. How the woman managed to balance on the things, she couldn't imagine.

Tuesday shoved a large plastic bowl into Millie's hands. "Green salad. Hope that's okay."

"Perfect," Millie assured her. "Justin, I have a feeling Albert would appreciate some help hooking up the TV in the parlor." Their private sitting room wasn't nearly big enough for all their guests to gather when it was time to watch the big race, so they'd decided to move it temporarily into the most comfortable room in the house.

"Sure thing." Justin disappeared in that direction while Millie led the others into the dining room.

Tuesday clomped along with an awkward gait, clearly unaccustomed to walking on stilts. It wouldn't be long before the massage therapist shed the shoes.

"Susan, is your daddy coming to the party?" Tuesday asked, a touch too eagerly. Though they'd become business partners during the renovation of the Day Spa, Tuesday had never hidden the fact that she found Thomas Jeffries to be an attractive man, and flirted outrageously at every opportunity.

Susan shook her head. "Afraid not. He was invited by a client to sit in the clubhouse at the Derby."

"Lucky man," said Violet, who overheard the comment as they entered the dining room. "That's the only way I'd go. They'll be packed in like sardines everywhere else."

The doorbell rang again, and a knot twisted in Millie's stomach. There were only two more guests who'd RSVP'd to say they'd come to the party. She cast a cautious glance at Violet as she heard the front door open and a familiar voice echo down the hallway.

"Yoohoo! Where is everybody?"

Violet recognized the newcomer instantly. She turned a wide-eyed stare on Millie. "You invited *her?*"

Before Millie could answer, the Thackers erupted into the room. Franklin had dressed for the occasion, though where he'd found pink-checkered trousers and that silky chartreuse shirt, she couldn't imagine. They looked like a golf outfit gone terribly wrong.

But it was Lulu who commanded attention. Wearing what looked like a towering fruit bowl on her head, she threw her arms wide and shouted, "Ta da! What do you think?"

"Oh my," said Susan, staring with a rather horrified fascination.

"It's quite elaborate," Millie managed.

Violet didn't bother to filter the heavy sarcasm out of her tone. "And completely appropriate if we decide to dance the Macarena."

"Exactly." Lulu beamed at her, oblivious to the cynicism. "And when we're finished dancing, we can eat it."

Tuesday approached to examine the headpiece closely and reached out a finger to touch an apple. "That's real fruit?"

"Sure is." Franklin plucked a grape off of his wife's head and popped it in his mouth.

"Oh, you!" Lulu awarded him a playful slap. "Would you stop eating my hat already?"

The pair guffawed, ending in unison snorts.

Franklin caught sight of Violet. "Hey, there's our invisible neighbor. What's shaking, Plum?"

A visible shudder rippled through Violet's frame. She detested the nickname Franklin had awarded her at their first meeting. Millie rushed in with a question.

"What's that you've brought?" She reached out to take the covered dish he carried.

"It's one of my specialties," Lulu answered. "Purple turnip pie." She addressed Violet. "Honey Bun wanted me to bring a plum cake, since we knew you would be here. But I figured everybody would bring desserts, so we compromised on purple turnips." She paused, and when Violet did not react, offered an explanation. "You know. Violet. Purple."

Millie didn't dare glance in Violet's direction.

❊

Al closed the door behind their guests and twisted the dead bolt. He wouldn't put it past Thacker to attempt reentry. He found it completely unfair that he was forced to suffer the man's presence all week long at the office and then be required to play host to him on the weekend too. But Millie insisted on inviting them. With a sigh, he shook his head. The things a man did for his wife.

He found Millie in the kitchen, trying to wrap a plate of mini hot browns in plastic wrap with one hand. Hurrying to her side, he took the roll from her. She edged sideways and began sealing the foil over the remains of the veterinarian's practically inedible Derby Pie. The corners of her lovely lips drooped, and there wasn't a sign of the dimples he loved.

"That was a good party," he ventured. "You did a great job."

"Thank you." The answer came by rote, full of despondency.

"I think everyone had a nice time."

"Everyone except Violet."

True. Violet had perched on a chair in the corner and sat without speaking anything but the occasional one-syllable answer to direct questions. Completely unlike her typical cliché-spouting self.

"She wasn't feeling well," he said, repeating Violet's excuse for leaving early.

Millie's mouth went rigid. "She felt just fine until Lulu got here. She was pouting, that's all."

Over the years Al had learned a thing or two about women in general and his wife in particular. When she was upset with something or someone, she did not want him to propose a solution, or sometimes, even offer an opinion. Doing so resulted in her ire redirecting itself toward the nearest target—him. A most unpleasant prospect. Time for the wonder-working words that applied to a multitude of situations.

"I'm sorry," he said with as much sympathy as he could pour into his tone.

Once again, the words did their job. She abandoned her struggles with the foil and, burying her face in his chest, threw her good arm around his neck. "Oh, Albert, I just hate conflict. With anyone, but especially with my best friend."

Al stroked her back in a soothing manner, much as he had done with Alison when some boneheaded boy had broken her teenaged heart. "I know." For good measure, he added another, "I'm so sorry."

His shirt muffled her words. "I never thought Violet could be mean-spirited. I know Lulu isn't the most likable person, but still."

No, definitely not likable, but Al could name at least one worse. The right to claim the title of Most Unlikable Person belonged to Lulu's husband. Still, living with the world's most irritating man would affect anyone. But now was not the time to voice the thought.

The sound of the doorbell sliced into the moment. Not one simple *ding-dong*, but an unending series of *ding-dong ding-dong ding-dongs*. Only one person would ring a bell with such annoying persistence.

"Thacker must have forgotten something," he said. "I'll see what he wants."

He left Millie in the kitchen and headed down the hallway, stopping to pick up a stray orange that must have rolled off Lulu's head. He opened the door, prepared to return the errant fruit to its owner, but halted when he caught sight of the person outside.

A large woman who carried her considerable girth on a sturdy frame that put her at eye level with Al stood on the porch. She wore a full-length maroon wool coat, though she must have been roasting from heat, and carried a black handbag looped over one arm. It was not merely her size that lent to her commanding presence, but a square jaw beneath tightly clamped lips and a pair of small, sharp eyes that traveled the length of him from top to bottom.

"Are you the butler?" The question sounded more like a demand.

"What?" Al was too confused to be offended. "Of course not. I'm Al Richardson. I live here."

"Richardson, you say?" She turned her head and shouted over her shoulder, "You may unload my bags."

For the first time, Al noticed a black limousine parked on the circular driveway near the bottom of the porch stairs. The trunk lid opened at a click from the driver's remote, and he began lifting out suitcases and setting them on the walkway.

"Hold up there," Al shouted, and then turned his attention back to the woman. "There's been some sort of mistake. Who are you?"

She tilted her head back, spearing him with an arrogant gaze down the not inconsiderable length of her nose. "I am Lorna Hinkle, and I am expected."

Al realized his mouth gaped open, and snapped it shut. Then he turned and shouted toward the kitchen for help.

"Millie!"

# Chapter Ten

"Why, yes, Mrs. Hinkle," Millie stammered, her head craned back to look up into the towering woman's face. "Of course we're expecting you."

"It's *Miss* Hinkle. I never married, and I don't hold with the new-fangled way of addressing unmarried women as *Ms.*" Her gaze shifted down the hallway, where Albert had disappeared to place an emergency call to Justin. "I had the impression my arrival took Mr. Richardson by surprise."

"To be honest, you've taken us both by surprise. We weren't expecting you quite so soon."

One penciled eyebrow arched. "I informed my future niece of my intention to arrive early in order to help with the preparations. Did she not relay the information?"

"She did," Millie rushed to say, lest she stir this imposing woman's ire against poor Susan. "But I assumed you'd arrive a few *days* early. The wedding isn't for another three weeks."

"An insufficient amount of time as it is, considering the lack of planning that has occurred to date." She made a pointed examination of the door frame and then asked, "Am I to be invited in, or am I expected to pitch a tent in the yard?"

"Oh!" Millie backed up and gestured. "Please forgive my lack of manners. Come in."

Before entering, Miss Hinkle turned to the limo driver. "Bring my bags inside."

She walked around the entry hall, her gaze sweeping the stairway, the polished wood floor leading down the hallway, the silk flower arrangement on a spindly-legged table Millie had found at the Peddler's Mall and refinished herself. With fresh eyes, Millie followed her gaze. Thank goodness she and Albert had cleaned for their Derby Party. The wooden banister shone in the waning sunlight that filtered through the lead crystal windows above the tall door. Not a speck of dust was in evidence, though…Millie stiffened. Was that a grape on the bottom step?

Albert returned from the direction of the dining room, which Millie remembered with horror still held unwashed dishes and the remnants of their party food.

"I called Justin. They'll be here in a minute," he announced. "Then we'll get this whole thing cleared up. Here!" He caught sight of the limo driver depositing a third and fourth suitcase in the hallway. "What are those?"

"My luggage, of course." Miss Hinkle spoke in the tone of one addressing an imbecile. "I clearly can't be expected to spend an extended period of time away from home without sufficient luggage." Her gaze once again circled the hallway, and Millie thought she spied the curling of one nostril. "Especially in the wilds of Kentucky."

"Extended period of time?" Alarm tinted Albert's question.

Millie laid a hand on his arm and hushed him with a look and a brief shake of her head. The last thing they needed at this point was Albert having hysterics in front of the B&B's first actual guest, no matter how unexpected her arrival.

"If I can bear it." Miss Hinkle's left nostril definitely curled. "I was given to understand that my nephew had performed renovation work here." She stepped sideways and ran a hand down the painted woodwork leading into the parlor, where Millie had purposefully left a gouge in the trim to retain a bit of the house's genuine historical feel. "Perhaps he hasn't had time to finish."

Millie was saved from replying when a car pulled up behind the limo. Doors on either side opened, and Justin and Susan emerged. Millie was sorry to see Susan had removed her hat—a hat was just the thing to impress a woman like Miss Hinkle—but she still looked lovely in her summery sundress.

Miss Hinkle's expression broke into one of pure delight as Justin rounded the front bumper and mounted the porch stairs two at a time.

"Justin!" The woman threw her arms wide to smother him in an embrace. "How like your dear mother you look. But with enough of your father to claim you as a Hinkle. It's been too long, far too long."

"Aunt Lorna, you look amazing." Justin stepped back, his hands still clasping the woman's arms, and beamed. "How do you manage to look the same today as you did five years ago?"

"Good genes, my boy." One heavily colored eyelid winked shut. "And you've inherited them too. But who is this ravishing young woman?" She released Justin and held her arms out to Susan, who approached with a hesitant step. "Susan? Why, you're as lovely as a Southern belle ought to be."

A becoming blush riding high on her cheeks, Susan was pulled into the circle of the woman's arms. "It's a pleasure to finally meet you, Aunt Lorna."

Millie's eye was drawn from the introductions to a point behind Miss Hinkle's back, where Albert stood waving his arms wildly above his head, his gaze fixed on Justin.

The young man got the point.

"Uh, Aunt Lorna, we're thrilled to see you of course," he said, "but we really weren't expecting you for another few weeks."

She drew herself up. "You need me, Justin." She grasped Susan's hand in one of hers and Justin's in the other. "This wedding needs me. I know you *think* you want a simple exchange of vows, but you must trust my expertise in this." During a pause she fixed first Justin and then Susan in a direct gaze. "Without me, your marriage is in jeopardy."

Susan cast a desperate glance toward Millie, clearly unable to reply.

Millie came to the rescue by stepping up to insert herself into the conversation. "We've plenty of time to discuss the wedding. For now, why don't we get you settled in?" She awarded Miss Hinkle her most welcoming smile.

"No. I can't let you do that." Justin looked up at his aunt. "Aunt Lorna, these are friends, and they aren't prepared to have a guest for three weeks. We can find you a nice hotel in Lexington. It's only a forty-minute drive."

"Forty minutes?" She rolled her eyes heavenward with an expansive gesture. "I'll have to hire a car, and think of the wasted time." Tucking Susan's hand into the crook of her arm, she awarded the girl a smile. "What if I stay with you, my dear? We can get to know each other."

Susan blanched. "But…that is to say, I…" A gulp, and then she recovered. "You're more than welcome to stay with me, but I live in a studio apartment and sleep on a fold-out couch. I'm afraid you'll find it cramped." She cast a glance at the five suitcases—the limo driver had just added another—lined against the wall.

"Oh." Stumped for a moment, the older woman looked at Justin and brightened. "I'll stay with you, then."

Justin sent an inquiring glance to his fiancé, and Susan gave a slight nod. "That would be great, Aunt Lorna. I only have a twin bed at the moment because our new bed won't be delivered for two more weeks. But you can have it, and I'll unroll a sleeping bag downstairs."

Millie could stand it no longer. With an apologetic glance at Albert, she stepped forward. "Nonsense. We have plenty of room here. Miss Hinkle, you will have the honor of being our first guest." She assumed what she hoped was a friendly smile. "It will give me a chance to practice my hostess skills."

"An excellent solution." The woman's chest expanded. "I've stayed in many a B&B, so I expect I can provide a great deal of assistance."

Her gaze roamed the hallway and her lips twisted. "Yes, a *great* deal of assistance."

While Millie reeled over the implied insult, the woman patted Susan's hand, which she still held in her clutches. "Tomorrow I'd like to take you to lunch. We have so much to discuss."

"I look forward to it," Susan replied, though she looked a bit stunned at the same time. Millie didn't blame her. Miss Hinkle was rather overwhelming.

"I'm sure you're tired from the trip," Millie said, more to rescue Susan than out of concern for Miss Hinkle. "Let me show you to your room."

"The travel was trying," Miss Hinkle admitted. "I hope the accommodations are appropriate for a lengthy stay, and especially at the price you quoted me."

Turning toward the stairs, Millie did a quick mental change. She'd planned to put Justin's aunt in the front room that he'd occupied until last week. But the one in the back of the house was bigger and the more stately of the three that were finished.

Miss Hinkle began to follow and then turned. She addressed Albert in an authoritative tone. "You may bring my bags."

Millie knew her husband well enough to recognize from his expression that he was about to utter an explosive response. She widened her eyes at him in an unspoken command to hold his tongue. Thankfully, Justin leaped toward the luggage.

"I'll do that."

With a resigned sigh, Albert joined the younger man in picking up a couple of suitcases. Millie led the parade up the stairs, turned left at the landing, and continued on to the room in the back. Thank goodness she had resumed her cleaning schedule yesterday and was confident that the wood on the dresser and night table shone. Though Albert had made an attempt the previous week, a man did not have the same eye for dust as a woman. When she opened the door, the faint scent of Tuesday's lemon cleanser wafted to her from the bathroom.

"We call this the Bo Peep room," she said, indulging in a brief smile. "Not officially or anything, but we've named every room after a Mother Goose nursery rhyme as we finish renovating it."

A wave of sadness threatened. She and Violet had decided on the names.

Miss Hinkle strode into the room and stopped in the center to turn in a circle, her sharp gaze taking in every detail. She approached the bed and tested the mattress with a hand, and then approached the small *en suite* and peeked inside. Breath caught in her chest, Millie awaited the verdict. Without a word, she went to one of the windows, pulled aside the pale pink curtain, and lifted the shade. A glimpse of the pond was visible through the branches of the walnut tree. Sunsets over the water were gorgeous to behold. Thanks to the April showers so plentiful in Kentucky, the grass was deep green all around the gazebo.

Miss Hinkle turned. "This tree obstructs the view. I'd prefer the room below this one."

Entering in time to hear the last comment, Albert dropped his burden and stiffened. "Below this is our private area. It is off-limits to guests." He speared Millie with a stern glare, as though he suspected she might have given away their bedroom had he not intervened.

Millie ignored him. "I assure you, Miss Hinkle, yours has the best view of all the guest rooms."

"Well." The woman sniffed. "I suppose the room with the second-best view is better than a hotel forty minutes away."

Justin arrived then and deposited the three suitcases he'd hefted upstairs on the floor beside the bed. "I've always liked this room. I wasn't sure about the paint color when you first picked it out, but on the walls it looks great." He gestured toward the crown molding, which was original to the house and still in excellent condition. "And the bright white on the molding really pops."

His aunt's demeanor changed in an instant. "Now that you point it out, dear boy, you're right." She awarded Millie a regal nod. "This room will do nicely."

Millie released a pent-up sigh. "Then we'll leave you to settle in. If there's anything you need, please let me know."

"I certainly will."

Millie didn't doubt that for an instant.

※

"I can't tell you how grateful I am," Justin whispered to Al. "I promise, I had no idea she planned to show up this early."

Though he would have liked to blame someone for this unexpected and *most* unwelcome disruption, Al knew the fault lay with the indomitable woman upstairs and not with the apologetic young man in front of him.

He managed a grudging reply. "We'll deal with it."

They stood on the front porch in the waning light. A chill had descended on the air, and Susan, dressed in a sleeveless sundress, shivered.

Justin put an arm around her shoulders. "We'd better get going. Since tomorrow's Sunday I'll have the day to devote to her. I'll pick her up in the morning and get her out of your hair."

Out of Millie's hair, more likely. If that woman was going to be here for three weeks, Al expected to spend a lot of time in the TV closet.

The young couple descended the porch steps and got into their car. With a farewell wave, Al watched them disappear down the long driveway before going inside.

He found Millie scurrying around the parlor, picking up leftover napkins and cups with one hand and setting them on a tray.

"Would you take this to the kitchen?" she asked. "And then help me clear the dining room. I'd hate for Miss Hinkle to see it looking like a disaster."

Before he lifted the tray, Al folded his arms across his chest and held her gaze. "Come clean, Mildred Richardson. Did you know she was coming early?"

"Not *this* early." Wide-eyed, she held up three fingers like a Girl Scout. "I expected her to come a few days before the wedding."

He believed her, of course. There could be no mistaking the shock they'd all exhibited when the arrogant Miss Hinkle arrived. Still, he couldn't help but remember that Millie had invited guests without consulting him. Were there other unpleasant surprises in store?

He narrowed his eyes. "Who else have you invited to stay with us?"

"Justin's cousin, and a man named Mark something who is a friend of Thomas Jeffries. Oh, and Thomas too. I've told him he'll have to stay in the Old King Cole room, which hasn't been renovated yet, and he's fine with that." She looked him in the eye without flinching. "They'll arrive the day before the wedding and leave the day after."

Almost a full house, and Millie with only one useful arm. Hopefully she would be fully recovered by then. In the meantime, he would no doubt be required to help in caring for the haughty woman upstairs.

Millie retrieved a dessert plate and fork from an end table and set it on the tray. "Look on the bright side. At least we'll be making some money."

Al brightened. "How much are we charging her?"

"One-fifty per night." A frown descended on her face. "Though maybe we should give her a discount since she's staying so long."

"She knew the price before she came." He shook his head. "Besides, she drove up in a limousine. I think she can afford it."

The sound of footsteps pounding down the stairs reached them.

"Mrs. Richardson!"

The shout sounded like a summons. Millie hurried to the parlor doorway. "We're in here."

Al picked up the tray and turned in time to witness Miss Hinkle's appearance.

"Mrs. Richardson," she repeated, this time in a stern manner that made Al fight the instinct to duck behind a chair. "That room will not do. There is no television! In fact, I inspected every guest room upstairs, and there are no televisions at all."

"Oh." Millie glanced at Al. "We've never discussed putting TVs in the rooms."

Another unbudgeted expense. Al straightened and addressed his reply to Miss Hinkle. "That's because we weren't expecting guests for three more weeks."

The woman's demeanor changed, and she turned a patronizing look on Millie. "Mrs. Richardson, you asked for my help in identifying deficiencies in your operation here."

Millie started to shake her head. "I don't—"

"Let me assure you," Miss Hinkle continued as if Millie had not spoken, "that a television in every room is absolutely essential. All the best bed-and-breakfasts have them. I absolutely insist on having one."

Millie's hand strayed to her mouth, and she cast a wide-eyed glance at Al. "Well, I suppose we could arrange—"

"Ah!" Miss Hinkle spied something and stalked across the room to stand in front of the large flat screen Al and Justin had set up for the Derby party. "This one will do nicely."

A series of outraged exclamations jumbled together on Al's tongue, but all he managed to say was, "*What?*"

"See that it's installed in my room tomorrow. And make sure I have access to the Shopping Channel."

She swept from the parlor without a backward glance.

Sputtering, Al set off after her, but Millie stepped in front of him.

"I'll scrounge up another television set tomorrow," she whispered. "Don't worry."

"We only have one cable box." He didn't intend the words to come out as a snarl, but Millie winced. Taking a deep breath, he said, "I'm sorry. But Justin and I had to move the cable box in here, and that only worked because there was already a connection. We'll have to call the cable company and have them install another connection upstairs. They'll probably charge us a fee."

"But, Albert, she's right. We'll need to do that eventually, so we might as well bite the bullet and do it now. In the meantime, we'll leave this one in here and she can watch the Shopping Channel in the parlor for a few days." The hand she placed on his arm was probably supposed to calm him. "I'm sure the cost won't come close to the price she's paying for a three-week stay."

Al allowed himself to be placated only because this wasn't Millie's fault. They were in this situation together. Thirty-eight years ago they'd taken a vow—for better or for worse. At the time he'd had no idea that the *worse* would involve an overbearing houseguest who hadn't been under his roof thirty minutes and had already overstayed her welcome.

# Chapter Eleven

The dishes finally cleaned and put away, the leftover colorful Derby napkins stored in a zipper baggie for next year, and every stray grape from Lulu's hat retrieved and disposed of, Millie and Al retired to their bedroom. Exhaustion dragged at her limbs, which made her nightly ablutions seem to take hours. She envied Al, who donned his pajamas, brushed his teeth, and slid between the sheets before she'd even managed to remove her makeup.

"Did you hear that?" His voice reached her from the bedroom.

Millie popped her head out of the bathroom. "Hear what?"

He sat up in bed, propped against a pillow, an old Zane Grey novel he'd read a dozen times in his lap. "The toilet flushed." He lifted a scowl toward the ceiling. "The water rushing through the pipes sounded like we should make a dash for Noah's ark."

She was too tired to try to placate him tonight. "Don't exaggerate, Albert."

As she returned to the bathroom, footsteps pounded from above. Goodness, they were quite loud. Perhaps she should look for a thick rug to put over the hardwood floor up there. Would that be enough to muffle the noise?

While running a brush through her hair, she traced Miss Hinkle's footfalls, her mind's eye supplying the woman's path from the bathroom to the dresser. A few moment's pause, and then another tromp across the room. To bed, hopefully? Or to the antique student's desk between the two windows? Whichever, silence descended, thank the Lord. Millie lined her toothbrush with minty gel and set about cleaning her teeth.

She'd just rinsed when Albert once again called to her.

"Millie!" This time his summons came in the form of a loud whisper.

Peeking into the bedroom, she found him sitting straight up, eyes wide, the novel forgotten. "I think she's coming."

Sure enough, the sound of heavy steps stomping down the hallway warned her moments before their bedroom door was thrown open without so much as a knock. Miss Hinkle, draped in yards of cotton and lace, stood in the doorway, her expression heavy with outrage.

"Mr. Richardson, at the prices I'm paying for lodging, I should at least be able to expect a reliable Internet connection. Yours is so slow it's practically unusable."

Albert, who had snatched the edge of the comforter up to his chin like a blushing maiden caught unawares in her nightie, stammered a reply that might have been, "Well…it's always been…that is to say…" He cast an alarmed glance at Millie in a clear plea for help.

Time to take control of the situation. Millie strode from the bathroom—thank goodness she'd not yet undressed—and crossed to the bedroom door. Taking Miss Hinkle by the arm, she led her firmly into the hallway and shut the door behind her.

"Thank you for letting us know about the Internet." She pasted on a genuine smile but instilled her voice with a purposeful edge of steel. "My husband is a computer specialist, so I'm sure he'll be able to address your concerns tomorrow."

"A specialist?" The woman gave a haughty sniff. "One would think he'd anticipate this problem, then."

*If we'd known you were coming, he might have.* Millie left the snarky thought unsaid. Albert probably wouldn't have thought about the

Internet connection any more than she'd thought about televisions in the rooms.

Instead, she firmed up her smile. One issue needed to be cleared up immediately. "Miss Hinkle, you're free to enjoy any part of the house or the grounds *except* our personal rooms. In the future, please knock before entering."

"I see." The thin lips twisted, and the skin surrounding her mouth settled into deep crevices that bore witness to the fact that the expression was a common one. With a slight nod, she said, "A reasonable request."

"Thank you."

She turned to go but then stopped. "I'm accustomed to having breakfast at ten. I assume I'll be served in the dining room?"

Until that moment Millie had not thought of breakfast. She felt like slapping her forehead. Of course she would need to serve breakfast. That was what the second *B* in *B&B* stood for. She took a quick mental inventory of the fridge. The remnants of the cheese tray, a few of Violet's country ham biscuits, and she was fairly sure she had at least a half-dozen eggs. She could easily whip up an acceptable omelet.

"Of course." She nodded. "But tomorrow is Sunday, so breakfast will be at nine o'clock. You're welcome to come to church with us."

"*Nine* o'clock?" A curling lip told Millie what she thought of the change in her routine, but she heaved a loud sigh. "I suppose I must be accommodating." Her gaze slid to the closed door behind Millie. "About a great many things, it appears."

Her head high, she turned and marched away.

Millie let herself into the bedroom to find that Albert had not moved from his previous pose. If she hadn't been so tired, she might have laughed at his indignant expression.

"Don't worry," she told him before he could complain. "I've told her our rooms are off-limits."

"Hmm." He relaxed enough to lower the comforter, though he

cast a suspicious glance toward the ceiling. "Tomorrow I'm putting a lock on our door."

Considering Miss Hinkle's demanding nature, Millie thought that an excellent idea.

※

Showered and refreshed, Al entered the kitchen with an attitude as bright as the morning sky. Amazing what a good night's sleep could do for a bad attitude. An enjoyable day stretched before him, without the presence of Miss Hinkle to spoil it. Today she would be Justin's headache.

Millie stood at the counter, her back toward him.

"Good morning, Mildred Richardson," he chirped.

She whirled, and in a flash Al revised his opinion of the day's prospects. Stress lines marred the usually smooth skin of his wife's forehead, and the corners of her mouth plunged downward. Something gooey dripped from her left hand, and in her right hand she held a blood-stained paper towel in the fingers that protruded from the brace on her right.

"Millie!" Al rushed across the room and gently took the injured appendage, pulling aside the paper towel to assess the damage. "What happened?"

Though her eyes remained dry, tears choked her words. "Have you ever tried to dice onions with your left hand? Or crack eggs, for that matter?"

Another drop of goo, which Al now identified as uncooked egg, dripped to the floor. An eggy mess covered the countertop around a bowl into which she had managed to get most of the eggs.

He inspected the cut on her forefinger. Only a shallow nick that had already stopped bleeding. Judging by the condition of the paper towel, he'd feared worse.

"Why didn't you wait for me?" He tore off another paper towel and used it to clean her left hand.

"I thought I could handle it myself." Her downcast expression tugged at his heart. "How many omelets have I made over the years?"

"Hundreds."

"At least. And the one I serve to my first guest is going to be awful." She sniffled. "We don't even have any mushrooms."

"I saw some out behind the gazebo yesterday. Want me to get them?"

A hint of his Millie appeared in the beginnings of a grin. "Don't be silly. They're probably poisonous toadstools."

He cast a meaningful glance toward the ceiling and their guest's bedroom. "And that would be a bad thing because...?"

"Oh, you." Grinning openly, she pointed toward the bowl of raw eggs. "See if you can fish the shells out of there, please." Her gaze took in his dress slacks and shirt. "Here. You'd better put on an apron first."

He did as instructed, donning the apron she removed from a drawer. Normally he would have balked at the frills, but he'd seen Millie frown too often recently. If wearing a fancy apron kept her happy, he'd do it.

She opened the back door to let Rufus in. The creature bounded toward him to prance at his side, waiting to be acknowledged.

"Yes, I see you," Al told the dog. "Good morning. I'm sure you've worked up an appetite chasing squirrels this morning."

Satisfied with a word directed his way, Rufus trotted to his bed in the corner and settled in for his first nap of the day.

"Oh!" Millie whirled, eyes wide. "Here she comes. Quick, go serve her coffee. Tell her breakfast will be ready shortly."

He would have argued that Millie could certainly handle a coffee-pot, but then he saw that she'd fixed up a tray with the fancy silver coffee service that had once belonged to her grandmother. She certainly couldn't carry a tray one-handed, so he swallowed a grumble, picked up the tray, and headed for the dining room.

He arrived at the same time as Miss Hinkle, whose eyebrows arched as she caught sight of him.

"This operation is smaller than I thought," she commented. "You not only act as butler and porter, you wait on the customers as well." She approached the table to stand beside the high-backed chair where Millie had laid a beautiful setting of china, shining silver, and an embroidered napkin. Miss Hinkle stood beside the chair and gave him an expectant look.

Jaws clamped tight, Al set the tray down and slid the chair out for her. For an instant, he considered jerking the chair backward as she lowered her considerable bulk into it. An uncharitable impulse reminiscent of his sons when they were adolescents. He slid it neatly beneath her.

Another pointed glance, this time toward the coffee urn. Al stiffened. Was he to pour for her as well? Did the woman expect him to spoon-feed her too?

Silent, he filled her coffee cup and returned the silver urn to the tray, which he slid close enough to be within her reach.

"I hope this is real cream." She pursed her lips, lifting the small silver pitcher. "Not that imitation stuff."

Though he had no idea what Millie had provided, he matched her haughty tone. "Of course it is. Breakfast will be ready soon."

As he turned to go, Rufus trotted into the room, his tail wagging in a friendly manner. He sauntered past Al, liquid brown eyes fixed on the visitor at the table.

"Ack!" A screech pierced the air, and Rufus skidded to a halt. "What is that?"

Al inspected the creature at his feet. "It's a dog."

Her gaze snapped to his face. "I *know* it's a dog. But what is it doing here?"

"It lives here."

Millie hurried into the room. "Is everything okay?"

Miss Hinkle extended an arm and pointed at Rufus, who for once was demonstrating a bit of sense and had remained statue-like at Al's side. "Mrs. Richardson, I trust you've taken precautions to keep the food preparation area clean and free of animal dander. I can't imagine what the health inspector said when he discovered that you have a creature given free run of the guest areas of the house."

Al risked a glance at Millie. From her expression, he knew the same thought had occurred to both of them. They hadn't considered contacting a health inspector.

Millie answered smoothly. "Miss Hinkle, I assure you my kitchen is completely sanitary. After all, Justin has been my guest for the past nine months, and has eaten countless meals in this house. I'm sure he'll vouch for the cleanliness of the facilities."

Brilliant move on her part to bring up the beloved nephew. Al awarded Millie an approving nod.

"Well." She fixed a withering gaze on Rufus. "I really must insist that you keep that canine out of the dining room. Its presence will quite ruin my appetite."

Though he may not have comprehended the words, the poor dog obviously picked up on the meaning. He turned and, tail drooping, slunk from the room.

Al followed, wishing that he, too, could be banned from the dining room for the duration of their guest's stay.

# Chapter Twelve

Susan rode in the backseat while Justin drove her car, glad for the space between her and Aunt Lorna. The cab of Justin's pickup wasn't big enough for the three of them, and of course his motorcycle wouldn't work. In fact, during the tour they'd given Aunt Lorna of their house, the sight of the bike in the garage had set off a twenty-minute harangue about the dangers of motorcycles and how she had barely slept a wink for three years since Justin bought his.

Their home had been declared, "Charming, if a bit cramped. When the children come along, you'll need to look for a more suitable place, of course." She had fixed Susan with a knowing glance. "And you shouldn't wait too long. You never know if you might experience difficulties." Which had sent heat flooding into Susan's face.

Since Aunt Lorna opted against attending church—"I'm far too exhausted to be put on display before the whole town my first day here"—they took her on a driving tour of Goose Creek. When they turned onto the northbound side of Main Street, Justin pointed out the Whistlestop Café on the corner.

"That's where we thought we'd go out for lunch after the ceremony. It's our favorite place in town to eat." He pulled into the parking lot and leaned slightly over the steering wheel, peering at the deep, rough-wooded front porch.

"It doesn't appear to be very well attended," Aunt Lorna said.

Seated behind her, Susan leaned toward the center of the seat to speak. "It's closed on Sundays. Most places in Goose Creek are."

The elderly woman twisted around to give her a stunned look. "Closed on Sundays? But think of the business they're losing."

"That's one thing I like about this place," Justin said. "The town rolls up the sidewalks on Sundays. People take their day of rest seriously. It's not like Boston."

"It certainly is not." Judging from her dry tone, Goose Creek compared unfavorably to Aunt Lorna's hometown.

Susan felt the need to defend her adoptive home. "But most of the people are so caring. My afternoon receptionist's little girl spiked a fever late one Sunday night. She called Mr. Cardwell, who opened his drugstore and brought her some medicine."

Her thin, overplucked eyebrows rose high. "The druggist made a home delivery?"

"Sure he did." Grinning, Justin put the car in reverse. "He knew Alice wouldn't feel comfortable leaving a sick child at home, even for a few minutes. So he did the neighborly thing and took it to her."

Aunt Lorna considered that in silence a moment, and then a frown appeared. "This place isn't at all suitable for a wedding reception. It's far too rustic."

Justin, who was turned in the driver's seat to watch out the rear windshield as he backed up, caught Susan's eye. She hadn't known her aunt-to-be long enough to contradict her, so the task fell to Justin. She told him so in a meaningful look.

"You're probably right," he told Aunt Lorna in his easygoing manner. "But we're not having a wedding reception. In fact, we're not really even having a wedding. We just want to go out for lunch with our family after a small, private ceremony."

From her vantage point in the backseat, Susan could only see Aunt Lorna's face in profile. Disapproval radiated from her clenched jaw, and Susan was grateful not to be on the receiving end of her direct stare. Feeling cowardly, she planted her face against the glass and left Justin to deal with his formidable aunt.

They drove up Main Street, executed a U-turn at the intersection of Walnut, and headed down the opposite side. Justin paused to point out Tuesday's Day Spa, which he had worked so hard to update and remodel.

"An unusual shade for a storefront," his aunt commented. A rather mild reaction, considering the source.

Justin laughed. "It fits the owner perfectly. You should stop in while you're here and let her give you a massage."

"Or a pedicure," Susan added. It would be impolite to sit in the backseat and let Justin shoulder the entire responsibility of conversation.

"Perhaps I will. And that reminds me, I need to do some shopping." A biting tone invaded her voice. "Obviously there's no suitable place in this town, Sunday or not."

"There's a Walmart in Frankfort," Justin suggested.

Laughter pealed through the car's interior. "Oh, dear boy, the very idea. I need a sturdy pair of *shoes*, not a toilet plunger. Apparently there's no public transportation system here, so I expect I'll be doing quite a bit of walking."

Susan bit her tongue before a ready comment escaped. *Walmart has shoes too.* Aunt Lorna appeared to be the kind of woman who paid more for a pair of shoes than Susan spent on her entire wardrobe.

"There are a several shoes stores in Fayette Mall," she suggested.

Aunt Lorna brightened. "There's a shopping mall nearby?"

"It's in Lexington, about a forty-minute drive," Justin warned.

"But it's huge," Susan said. "It's the biggest mall in the state of Kentucky."

An actual giggle bubbled in the woman's throat, and she rubbed her hands. "Forty minutes is perfect." She half-turned in her seat and settled her back against the door to peer at Susan around the headrest.

"It will give me time to get to know my new niece better. And to discuss a few simple ideas I have about the wedding."

She gave a broad smile, which Susan managed to return.

❄

By the time they parked the car in front of Millie's house, Susan's feet hurt so badly she half considered putting in a call to Tuesday for an emergency foot massage. Aunt Lorna leaped out of the car and bounded up the porch steps with the energy of a six-year-old hyped up on Halloween candy.

Alone in the car for a moment, Justin turned around and looked at Susan. Though it did not seem possible, the love of her life had aged ten years in the span of six hours. The skin around his eyes sagged, his shoulders stooped, and he appeared to be having trouble keeping his eyes open. Even his hair seemed to have lost the strength to hold a curl and lay flat against his ears.

"What was so fascinating in that one store to keep her inside for an hour?"

"Cookware." With an effort, she filtered the sharp edge of resentment out of her voice. At least he'd been able to rest after he collapsed on a bench in the center of the mall and refused to budge. Aunt Lorna wouldn't hear of Susan failing to accompany her while she inspected every single item in the nearly one hundred stores they visited.

"You mean like pots and pans?"

"Yes." Susan gave into an open-mouthed yawn. "And cookie sheets and spatulas and canister sets and…" She flipped her fingers in the air. "Who knows what else? My eyes glazed over halfway through. I think she bought us one of everything in there. We're going to have to build an addition on the kitchen to hold all that stuff. Only don't tell her that, or she'll hire an architect to draw up blueprints."

"She's generous. I'll give her that."

"A bit too generous, don't you think?" She cast a glance toward the

B&B's door, which stood open. "It's kind of embarrassing to have someone buy so many gifts for us."

"She's finally getting a niece, another girl in the family. Let her spoil you if it makes her happy." Justin extended a hand, and she placed hers into it, reveling in the warmth of his touch. "If I were rich, I'd do the same."

Which reminded her of a question she'd pondered throughout the day. "All that stuff she bought today must have cost a fortune. Where did she get her money?"

"She worked as an executive assistant for some big corporation up in Boston until she retired. Never married, and she still lives in the house my great-grandfather built when she was a girl. It was paid for decades ago, I'm sure. No mortgage, no car, no family to spend her money on. I'll bet she still has the first dime she ever made."

"Well, she won't have it long if she keeps buying everything in sight." A movement caught her eye. Aunt Lorna and Al descended the porch while Millie stood watching from the doorway. "There they are. Pop the trunk."

Justin did, and then exited the car. Susan rifled through the shopping bags filling the backseat beside her until she found the one from the first department store they'd visited. What would Millie think about Aunt Lorna's gift? Grabbing one of the bags by the handles, she opened her door and stood, wincing when her feet took the burden of her weight.

"Carefully, please." Aunt Lorna stood off to one side, watching Al and Justin lift the heavy carton out of the trunk. "Seven years is a long time to suffer for one clumsy mistake."

"Yikes." Al adjusted his grip on the edges of the large, flat box. "What's in here? Bricks?"

"It's a mirror." Justin swung so they could both walk forward up the stairs. "A big, heavy one."

Aunt Lorna turned toward Millie, who had exited the house and stood watching the procedure from the covered porch. "My dear Mrs.

Richardson, you will simply adore it. It's a regent's mirror based on an eighteenth century English antique, beautifully beveled and in such a gorgeous bronze that I knew the moment I saw it that it *must* go in the Bo Peep room. It's absolutely perfect and far more suitable than the small one hanging there."

Millie's jaw dangled, and Al halted midstep. "You bought a mirror for our house?"

Frowning, Aunt Lorna pointed toward Al. "Watch where you're going. Take care on those stairs."

They turned the box sideways to enter the house and passed out of view.

Aunt Lorna turned. "Susan dear, would you bring one of the— ah. You've got it."

Susan relinquished the voluminous shopping bag and followed Aunt Lorna to the porch, her expression carefully impassive while the second gift was bestowed.

"This is for you."

Her expression stunned, Millie stammered, "I—don't know what to say." She peered into the bag. "What is it?"

Aunt Lorna set the shopping bag on the porch and extracted an item. "Towels."

"But we have plenty of towels." She lifted a questioning gaze to Susan, who shrugged.

"Not like these," Aunt Lorna insisted. "Feel that." Obediently, Millie rubbed a hand over the towel. "It's Egyptian velour jacquard. I've bought you a dozen, with matching hand towels and facecloths."

Millie snatched her hand away. "They must have cost a fortune. I can't accept them."

"Nonsense." The older woman replaced the towel in the bag. "A quality B&B must have quality bath linens. No offense, dear, but the towel I used this morning practically took the top two layers of skin off."

Clearly taken aback, Millie remained speechless. Having been placed in the same position many times throughout the day, Susan felt a rush of sympathy for her.

"Now, before the men return, I have a matter I'd like to discuss." Aunt Lorna looped an arm through Susan's and pulled her toward the house. "Just us girls."

They entered the parlor, and Aunt Lorna pulled the heavy wooden door shut behind them. Turning, she dusted her hands. "Now, about the wedding reception."

*Oh, no.* A wail of despair nearly escaped Susan's lips. Throughout the day whenever Aunt Lorna brought up the wedding, Justin had deftly turned the conversation. Now it was Susan's turn to have her willpower put to the test.

"There isn't going to be a reception." She kept a smile in place. "Justin and I agreed on that from the outset."

"Oh come, my dear." Aunt Lorna shook her head slowly and fixed Susan with a pitying look. "Men simply don't understand a woman's desires in matters like this." Before Susan could voice an argument, she turned to Millie. "How about you, Mrs. Richardson? Did you have a reception when you married Mr. Richardson?"

With a nervous glance toward Susan, Millie nodded. "Yes, but we had a rather large wedding, so it was expected."

"And your daughter?" When Millie looked surprised, Aunt Lorna smiled. "I saw the pictures in the dining room. A lovely girl, and such a beautiful, simple dress she wore. I especially liked the close-up of her and her husband's hands holding the knife poised above their wedding cake, their gold rings shining."

A misty look appeared on Millie's face. "She was a beautiful bride."

"And where was that reception held? From the photo I thought it might have been at someone's home."

Millie nodded. "Mine. Not this one, but where we lived before. Alison married in a hurry because her husband was being deployed overseas. Still, we managed to host a very nice reception for a few cl—oh." With a glance toward Susan, she lifted her good hand to cover her mouth.

Aunt Lorna didn't miss a beat. "I'm sure it was splendid, and that your daughter was grateful."

An apology stole over Millie's features. "She was, actually. At first she didn't want photos taken, but many times she's told me how glad she is to have them."

Susan gulped. On the mantel at Daddy's house stood a treasured picture of her mother in a lovely wedding gown, gazing up into her new husband's face. How many hours over the years since Mom's death had Susan spent staring at that photo? Would her own daughter one day ask to see pictures of her parents on their wedding day?

*Stand firm.* She could almost hear Justin's voice. *Don't give in.*

"I'm sure we can get someone to snap a picture of us in the pastor's office," she said. "Uncle Mark will do it."

"No doubt that will be very nice." Aunt Lorna's tone sounded as though she doubted it. "But why not there?" She pointed toward the fireplace along the back wall. "Such a beautiful room, and that carved mantel was absolutely made for a bridal photo."

As one, Millie and Susan faced the fireplace. The mantel *was* gorgeous, and the ornate vase Millie had placed on one end sparkled with light from the crystal chandelier.

"You could swing by here when you leave the pastor's office." Millie spoke slowly. "Pose for a picture or two. Another place I've always thought would be lovely for a bridal photo is the staircase in the front hall."

"Well…" Thoughts whirled in her head. Was there anything wrong with having a picture or two taken in this beautiful house? After all, Justin had done a lot of work here and even lived here for almost a year. In a way it would be kind of appropriate. "I think that would be okay."

"Wonderful!" Aunt Lorna beamed. "You won't be sorry, Susan dear."

She opened the door and swept out of the room, Millie in tow.

Susan followed more slowly. What was this lingering sense of failure? She'd agreed to a couple of photos. That actually wasn't even a change to any of the arrangements she and Justin had made. And she *did* want pictures of her wedding day.

Still, she couldn't help thinking about Justin's warning. She'd just cracked open the door, and Aunt Lorna had planted a sturdy foot in the opening. What was next on the determined lady's agenda? St. Paul's Cathedral?

# Chapter Thirteen

Yes, tomorrow will be perfect." Speaking into the receiver, Millie jotted a note on the calendar. "I appreciate your fitting me in."

She hung up the phone and finished writing *Cable installation—afternoon* in her awkward left-handed script. That would make Miss Hinkle happy. And Justin, who was working on a house in Frankfort, had promised to stop by Walmart and buy a television to go in the Bo Peep room. She'd given him a budget and told him to purchase the best one to be had for that amount of money. No doubt he would refuse payment, but Millie planned to insist. She patted her pocket, where she'd tucked cash from her secret stash. If necessary, she would hide the money in his toolbox when he wasn't looking.

Normally she would have been stationed behind the veterinary clinic reception desk at this time of the morning, but last night she'd called Alice and asked her to fill in for the foreseeable future. The young mother had been embarrassingly eager, which left Millie with a guilty feeling in her stomach. Albert might grumble about the lost income, but as the sole supporter of her five children, Alice needed the money far more than Millie.

She caught sight of Rufus napping on his cushion. "Oh…before I forget."

He raised his head, watching as she rummaged in her purse for the small notebook she carried to jot down reminders. Flipping to the end of a to-do list that had more items crossed off than not, thank goodness, she wrote *Call Angela Parrish.* Though she knew Angela only casually, Angela's son worked for the county's public health department. Perhaps he could pull some strings to arrange a health inspection of her kitchen. How embarrassing not to have thought of that earlier. Hopefully Angela's son could convince the inspector to overlook the lapse this once.

The doorbell rang. Millie glanced at the clock. Nine twenty. Still a while before she needed to get breakfast for Miss Hinkle. Thank goodness the woman slept late. If Albert had to face her over breakfast every morning for the next three weeks, Millie feared he might find temporary lodgings for the duration.

She hurried down the hallway to forestall a second ring that might awaken her guest.

A less-than-pleasant surprise awaited her on the porch. Frieda Devall stood with her purse straps clutched in both hands, wearing a floppy straw hat and a shamefaced expression.

"I came to apologize," she said before Millie could come up with a safe greeting. "And to ask a favor."

The need for a favor explained the apology from the normally stiff-necked woman. Assuming a gracious smile, Millie opened the door wider. "Come in. There's fresh coffee in the kitchen."

While Millie retrieved a clean mug, Frieda selected a chair at the kitchen table. Though her guest fidgeted with her hat and her purse, Millie did not indulge in the small talk she knew would set Frieda at ease. Still offended on Lulu's behalf, she was determined that any ice-breaking must originate with the offender.

When steaming mugs sat between them, Frieda finally spoke. "Violet and I talked after church yesterday."

The opener took Millie by surprise. Many times on a Sunday afternoon, Violet joined Millie and Al for a lunch of leftovers. Of course yesterday Violet had been absent from Sunday school, had selected a seat on the opposite side of the sanctuary for the service, and had avoided looking in Millie's direction. Yet she had spoken with Frieda?

Stinging, Millie stirred a spoonful of sweetener into her coffee simply to give herself something to look at besides Frieda's sharp-eyed gaze. "Did you?"

"She told me you're still angry over the whole Main Street Manager thing."

Millie chose her words carefully. "I'm more offended than angry. You have no idea how hard Lulu has worked on this application. To deny her the opportunity to head up the program once we're approved is unfair."

"*Lulu* has worked hard?" Frieda leaned forward and caught Millie's eye. "From what I understand, you've worked just as hard. Lucy Cardwell told me you did all the talking when the pair of you met with her and Leonard to get their support, and John Hockensmith said the same thing. I understand you even put in calls to Carl Sickmiller and Randy Offutt about the vacant buildings they own."

"Lulu's idea," Millie hurried to say. She paused for a sip of coffee and to gather her thoughts. "It's true I've handled most of the talking, but Lulu is excellent at written communication, and when it comes to research, she's amazing. She's unearthed details I wouldn't even know to look for. When we went to Carrollton—"

"So she's a good research assistant." Frieda dismissed Millie's argument with a flick of her fingers. "She'll be a great help to the Main Street Manager in that capacity."

Millie set her mug down a little more forcefully than she intended. Coffee sloshed over the side and onto the vinyl tablecloth. "Where is this coming from? According to Albert, at the last celebration committee meeting you applauded Lulu for volunteering."

"Nobody else wanted to do it."

Aha. Now they were getting to the truth of the matter. "And now someone has come forward to volunteer? Someone you think would be more suitable for the job? Cheryl Lawson, perhaps?"

The name of the instigator failed to produce the anticipated response. Frieda replied calmly. "Cheryl brought up a valid point, that the Main Street Manager should be someone with a longer history in Goose Creek than a few months. But she's not interested in the job. We have another candidate we think is far more suited to the position than Lulu Thacker."

With rigid self-control, Millie managed to ask in a calm manner, "And who is *we*?"

"The Cardwells, John, and Randy." She ticked off a finger with each name. "I couldn't get hold of Carl, but I'm confident he'll agree. Plus, the other members of the committee, Phyllis and Tuesday."

Millie sat back in her chair. Tuesday? She studied Frieda's face but could detect no trace of insincerity. How had she managed to recruit Tuesday in her effort to cut Lulu out of the manager job? The new candidate must be someone highly thought of by the massage therapist and the others.

The answer came in a flash. Abruptly, Millie rose, her chair legs scuffing across the floor with a loud scrape. Taking her overly sweet coffee to the sink, she poured it out while a battle erupted in her mind.

Frieda spoke from the table. "We'd like you to take the job, Millie. You've lived in Goose Creek your entire life."

"Not really," she said automatically. "I moved to Akron for seven years when Albert and I first married."

"So you've lived here *most* of your life. The point is, you know the town and the people. You're one of us. You'll be the perfect Main Street Manager."

Millie turned on the faucet and watched water fill her mug. The ambition she'd managed to overcome ten days ago resurrected from somewhere deep inside. When she'd first discovered the existence of the Main Street Program, she'd seen herself as its manager. Frieda was right. Her history with the town and the people made her the perfect person to run the program. People would listen to her because she was one of them. A Creeker. Especially now that she was a business owner too.

Albert's words came back to her. She spoke without turning. "I already have a job. Two, in fact. I don't have time for a third."

"I was under the impression that you planned to quit working at the veterinary clinic when the B&B opened."

Millie bit her lip. She'd made no secret of that fact.

Frieda continued. "Once the program gets going, I can't imagine it will be a full-time job. It probably won't take more than a few hours a week. Think of the exposure you'll gain for your B&B with such a prominent position of leadership in the Creek."

That was true, and one of the reasons she'd originally wanted the job.

Water flowed over the sides of the mug and trickled down the drain. What would Lulu say when she heard the committee's recommendation? Oh, Millie knew what she would *say*. She would be thrilled for her new friend and would exclaim that Millie was far better suited than she. But her feelings on the matter would be different. Would she feel that Millie had betrayed her?

Millie twisted the knob to shut off the water. She would not betray a friend, not even for her own ambition.

Holding her head high, she faced Frieda. "I'm not interested. Lulu has the time to devote. She has an in-depth knowledge of the program and has started developing relationships with other communities around the state." That last wasn't exactly a lie. She'd at least met the other Main Street Managers, even though she'd made a less than stellar impression on some of them. "I'll assist her however I can to make sure Goose Creek's program is successful."

There. Though the offer stung, at least being Lulu's assistant was less painful than the miserable guilt Millie would feel at betraying a friend.

Apparently her answer was not the one Frieda expected. The owner of the Freckled Frog stared at her, mouth hanging open.

The silence was broken by the sound of a toilet flushing upstairs and water rushing through pipes.

Millie smiled brightly. "I hate to rush you away, but my guest will be wanting her breakfast soon."

Frieda rose and, still silent, gathered her hat and purse. She allowed Millie to escort her down the hallway and open the front door.

She turned in the doorway. "If you change your mind—"

"I won't." Millie smiled to soften her firm words.

Lips pressed tightly together, Frieda gave a nod. "Then I'll see you at the committee meeting on Thursday."

After closing the door, Millie paused with her hand on the knob to draw in a deep breath. There it was. She'd driven a stake through the heart of her aspirations to civic leadership. What a surprise that she didn't feel even a smidge of regret.

Smiling, she headed for the kitchen for a one-handed attempt at scrambled eggs.

❋

By Wednesday Millie had become adept at left-handed egg cracking. She hummed a tune as she dished a large portion of fluffy eggs onto a plate, added four sausage links, wheat toast, and garnished tomato slices—cut by Albert before he left for work this morning—with a sprig of fresh parsley. Quite an attractive presentation, if she did say so. She picked up the plate and headed for the dining room.

Rufus interrupted a snore to leap to his feet.

"Stay," she commanded in the firm tone that told him she meant business.

The poor dog's ears drooped. He slumped back to his cushion and collapsed with a forlorn sigh.

Footsteps heralded her guest's approach as Millie slid Lorna's plate—they'd achieved first-name basis just yesterday, though Albert had not yet been granted the privilege—onto the lacy place mat at her usual seat. Whirling to the gleaming sideboard, she retrieved the silver jam bowl filled with homemade apple butter and placed it within her guest's reach. When Lorna entered, Millie was filling her china cup with coffee.

"Good morning," she chirped. "Did you sleep well?"

"Passably," came the grudging reply. Lorna approached the table, eyeing her breakfast with a lack of enthusiasm. "Scrambled eggs again?"

Chagrined, Millie examined the beautifully arranged plate of food. "You don't like scrambled eggs?"

"Not a consistent diet of them." Heaving a resigned sigh much like Rufus's a moment before, Lorna seated herself and picked up a fork. "My dear, if you want to operate a quality B&B, you really must broaden your menu."

Millie clamped her mouth shut before she could point out that the breakfast meat had changed every day, from bacon to sausage to sliced ham, and today's links. And yesterday she'd included a side of fresh melon. But it was true that scrambled eggs had made a consistent appearance, since she did not yet trust herself to flip an over-easy without breaking it.

"Of course you're right." Millie set a second silver bowl beside the apple butter, this one filled with strawberry jam. "I'll come up with something different tomorrow. Perhaps a continental breakfast for a change?"

Lorna halted in the act of spreading her napkin across her lap to award a disdainful stare. "At the prices you charge?" She smoothed the linen with a prim gesture. "I think something rather more substantial than a donut is to be expected."

Thus chastened, Millie turned to head for the kitchen.

"Millie dear, I hoped to speak with you about the wedding reception."

The nonexistent reception had become a favorite topic. Each evening after work Justin appeared to take his aunt out to dinner, and the poor boy had confessed last night that Lorna's constant badgering was beginning to wear on him.

Lorna spoke while spreading jam on her toast. "Now that I've had the opportunity to sample the wares of the only two restaurants in town, I've come to the conclusion that neither is an appropriate venue."

Millie slipped her good hand into the sling to rest on top of the other. "I wasn't aware that Susan and Justin had changed their plans about having a reception."

"Merely a matter of time. I came all the way from Boston to help plan a wedding, and I don't intend to be thwarted." She balanced the knife on the edge of her plate. "Since the wedding party will come here after the ceremony, I see no reason why we can't host a small reception. After all, you have a lovely home."

Millie glanced around the dining room at the high ceilings, the vintage chandelier, the elegant wood trim. This room would be the perfect place to lay out a spread of tasty treats for a reception. Guests could take their plates into the parlor, or if the weather was nice, out onto the veranda.

But she refused to pit herself against the young couple of whom she'd grown nearly as fond as her own children.

"Though I agree that the house is perfectly suited, I'm hardly in a condition to host a reception." She extracted her injured wrist from the sling and held it aloft as proof.

"That's what caterers are for."

Millie shook her head. "Even if you could convince Susan and Justin to agree to a reception, I doubt they'll stand for a catered event."

A thoughtful expression settled on Lorna's face. "You're right, of course." Then she brightened. "No matter. I'll help. And surely you have friends who would pitch in. I'm not talking about a six-course meal, just a few tidbits. And a cake, of course."

A wave of sorrow washed over Millie. Normally Violet would leap in with enthusiasm, but unless something changed between them, Millie wouldn't ask. Still, she did have other friends. Lulu, for instance. A laugh escaped her lips at the thought of asking Lulu to bake a wedding cake. What unusual ingredient would she include? Broccoli, perhaps?

Mistaking the reason for her laughter, Lorna smiled broadly. "You agree then?"

The wedding would take place in seventeen days. Certainly Millie's wrist would be well enough to cook by then. Already she'd regained some use, as long as she acted with discretion. And it would be fun to host a small reception.

"If you can convince them," Millie told Lorna, "then I agree."

"Excellent. After breakfast we'll start pla—"

The doorbell chimed.

"Enjoy your breakfast," Millie told Lorna as she headed in that direction.

A pair of delivery men stood outside. Behind them, a large box truck stood on the driveway with its engine running. The logo on the side read Haverty's Furniture.

A dark-haired man looked up from his clipboard. "You Mrs. Richardson?"

"Yes."

"We're here with your delivery."

Millie shook her head. "There's been a mistake. I didn't order anything."

"No mistake." Lorna's voice announced her entry to the hall. She addressed the men. "Take it upstairs. The room on the far left."

While the two returned to their truck, Millie stared at Lorna. "Is it a wedding present for Susan and Justin?"

"No, dear, it's a gift for you."

Surprised, Millie laid her hand across her collarbone. "Me?"

"And your future guests. The Bo Peep room desperately needs a comfortable chair. My back can't take another evening in that hard-backed desk chair." She retreated a step to allow entry to the two men who carried a huge wing-backed recliner covered in plastic. "Since Justin installed that device to boost the wireless signal, I'm finally able to get online upstairs. I found this chair at a store in Lexington and decided it will go beautifully with the new mirror. The dark rose print will make a perfect contrast to the color you selected for the wall, don't you think?"

"But, Lorna, I don't have any money in my budget for new furnishings."

"I said it's a *gift*, dear." She started up the stairs, but paused. "Oh, and the rug should arrive tomorrow. I found a beautiful one on the Shopping Channel night before last. The hardwood floors are exquisite, of course, but a bit too cold for my tastes."

Without waiting for a response, she swept after the delivery men. Moments later her voice drifted down the stairs, directing the placement.

※

Susan picked at her salad, unable to force a bite down her throat until they'd put this business about the reception to bed. The waiter hovered nearby with the iced tea pitcher, ready to leap in as soon as Aunt Lorna's glass showed signs of emptying. No doubt the poor young man was not eager for a repeat of the sharp reprimand he'd received when he failed to notice her empty glass earlier.

"It's not as though you'd be putting Mrs. Richardson to any trouble," Aunt Lorna said. "She assured me this morning she'd be delighted to host the reception."

Seated to her right, Justin picked up his burger in both hands and planted his elbows on either side of his plate. "Being a bother to Millie or you or anyone else isn't the issue. We've talked it over, and we don't want anything formal."

"It needn't be formal." The older woman glanced around the Whistlestop's dining room, distaste twisting her lips. "Clean would be nice."

"This place is plenty clean," Justin assured her. "Just because the walls and beams are rough wood doesn't mean they're not clean. And the food's good. How's your chicken?"

She speared a morsel and inspected it. "Acceptable," she finally admitted, and placed the bite in her mouth.

"There you go. Clean, good, and close to the church." Justin grinned sideways at Susan before biting into his burger.

Susan managed a weak smile. Millie's B&B was also close to the church, but she kept the comment to herself.

Aunt Lorna might have read her mind. "Everything is close to everything else in this town. The Richardson home is only a mile or so away." She directed her attention to Susan. "You did say location was the main reason you selected this establishment. That the food was not of the primary consideration."

Clearing her throat, Susan cast a sideways glance at Justin. "That's true. We really don't want a fancy meal. Just a quiet celebration after a private ceremony."

Thin eyebrows arched high. "Quiet and private?"

The noise in the café came suddenly into focus. The chatter from a dozen or so tables filled the room. Utensils clanked against plates, and from the direction of the kitchen came the metallic clang of a pan. Glancing around, she exchanged a distracted smile with several familiar faces. This was only Wednesday, and the place was half-full with people she recognized. On Saturdays the Whistlestop overflowed with Goose Creek residents. No doubt they would each want to stop by the table of the town veterinarian and her new husband to congratulate them and wish them well. Their quiet, private family meal would be anything but.

A perceptive gleam appeared in Aunt Lorna's eyes. She took the napkin from her lap and dabbed at her lips. "If you'll excuse me, I'd like to powder my nose." She slid out of the booth. "Perhaps you two would like a moment to discuss the matter privately."

When she moved out of earshot, Justin heaved a laugh. "She's a piece of work, isn't she?"

Rolling a cherry tomato to the side of her plate, Susan didn't meet his eye. "She does have a point about this place not being private. Or quiet either."

Justin set his burger down and turned sideways on the bench. "I don't believe it."

"What?"

"She's getting to you."

"No she's not." But her voice held a note of hesitancy.

"Yes she is. She got you with the pictures, so now she's onto the food."

Susan looked up quickly. "It has nothing to do with food. I don't care if we don't have anything to eat at all. Except…" She bit her lip.

Justin ducked his head to catch her eye. "Except what?"

"Well, it might be nice to have a cake." She glanced up. "Nothing fancy, just something to…you know…cut." She swallowed. "Together."

"Suz, listen to me." He picked up her hand and sandwiched it between his. "You're standing at the top of a slippery slope. Every step you take puts you in danger of a downhill tumble, straight into Aunt Lorna's plans."

"You make her sound like a devious schemer."

He cocked his head. "Devious? No. But she's a master manipulator. Don't get me wrong, she means well. But keep in mind that she's an old maid who never married. She's probably trying to plan her own dream wedding and project it onto you."

His words made her grin. "Listen to you spouting armchair psychology."

He shrugged. "It's true."

"Still, some things she says make sense." She chewed on the inside of her cheek. "To be honest, I think I'd rather go back to Millie's and have a sandwich and a piece of cake with our four family members than come here and be on display for the whole town."

"Then that's what we'll do." He lifted his hands to cup her face. "Whatever my bride wants, my bride gets."

Was there a luckier girl anywhere? Leaning forward, she planted a kiss on his lips. In the second that followed, the noise level in the restaurant rose, and she heard a few indulgent chuckles from the onlookers. Proof that there was no privacy to be had at the Whistlestop Café. She'd made the right decision.

But from here on, she needed to hold firm. Maybe now that Aunt Lorna had won two major victories, she'd be satisfied. Susan hoped so, because the changes in their plans stopped here.

*Chapter Fourteen*

The addition of a gavel gave the celebration committee meeting an official feeling that had not been present the last time Millie attended. Frieda applied the mallet with energy to a round sounding block, filling the small meeting room with an unnecessarily sharp sound that stung Millie's ears. Across the conference table Phyllis winced. Beside her, Lulu continued knitting as though she hadn't noticed. In fact, she appeared to be completely unaware of the nearly palpable tension that filled the room even more stingingly than the pounding of the gavel.

After having spent two weeks with her new friend, Millie knew better. The speed with which the knitting needles flew was an accurate barometer to Lulu's anxiety level.

"Gotcha a new toy?" Tuesday asked.

Frieda held the gavel aloft for their inspection. "One of my vendors carves them by hand. I doubt if there'll be much call for them at the Frog, but I kind of liked the look of the thing."

In no mood for chitchat about a wooden hammer, Millie cleared her throat. "Can we get started? I've got a million things on my plate today, so I hope we can finish quickly."

Not exactly the truth. In fact, Lorna had arisen early and without too much grumbling in order to ride into town with Lulu and Millie. Though what she intended to see in tiny Goose Creek Millie hadn't the faintest idea. By the time this meeting ended, she would probably be chomping at the bit to get back to the B&B and her beloved Shopping Channel.

"Of course." Frieda awarded her a chilly nod. "I've got Cheryl watching my shop, so I don't want to impose on her too long. Before we get to the major discussion of the morning, I'd like to report that the Biscuit Burners Bluegrass Band has declined our invitation to play at the anniversary celebration. Apparently they've gone on an indefinite hiatus."

"Oh." Tuesday slumped in her chair with a pout. "I listened to them on YouTube and was looking forward to hearing them in person."

"Do we have a volunteer to contact the next band on our list?" Frieda put on a pair of reading glasses and examined her spiral notebook. "The Buzzard Boys?"

Phyllis raised a hand.

"Thank you." Frieda jotted a note and then removed her glasses. "Unless there's any other new business, I think we can move on to the Main Street Program application."

Lulu set down her knitting and extracted a thick envelope from her bag. She caught Millie's eye with an unspoken question as she slid out a stack of documents. Millie nodded for her to take the lead. They'd discussed their presentation to the committee, and though Lulu preferred to sit silently knitting, Millie refused. Lulu needed to demonstrate that she was in control.

"I hope you've all had a chance to look at the application we emailed yesterday. But just in case, we brought hard copies."

"Thank you," Tuesday said, extending her hand to take one. "I never remember to check my email. Don't know why I even bother to have a computer."

"I studied it last night," Phyllis said. "It was very thorough. You two have done a great job."

"Lulu wrote the entire report herself." Millie cast a quick glance toward Frieda.

"Wow." Tuesday flipped to the second page, eyes moving as she scanned. "You've covered everything. There are sections here on Organization, Promotion, Design, and Economic Restructuring."

"That's the required four-point approach," Lulu explained. "I didn't come up with that breakdown myself."

Millie gave her a stern look. They'd rehearsed the "talking points" for this meeting, as Albert called them. One thing she had stressed was Lulu's self-conscious habit of apologizing for what she considered her own weaknesses. Rather an unusual trait for one so brash and, well, it must be said—lacking in tact. But people often reacted to stress in odd ways.

"Still, you've outlined an approach that the city council is sure to approve." Phyllis turned a smile on her. "I think this will be a slam dunk at tonight's council meeting."

"There's one thing missing here." Tuesday cast an apologetic glance toward Millie. "The name of the person we're recommending for Main Street Manager."

An awkward silence settled over the meeting. Lulu engaged in a close inspection of a paper clip while Phyllis flipped through the pages of the application too quickly to read them.

Millie pointedly did not look at Frieda. The time had come to break her silence. She directed her comment to Tuesday. "Since there appears to be some disagreement about the person this committee will recommend, Lulu preferred to leave a blank for us to fill in after we've discussed the matter. Against my advice, I should add."

"You think we should recommend Lulu," Phyllis said, the statement falling flat.

"I do." Millie held her head high. "Given the amount of work she's put into this application, I have no hesitation in saying she's the person best suited for the job." A glance at Tuesday's thoughtful expression, and Phyllis's apologetic one, sent the rehearsed speech out of her mind. She pounded the table with a fist. "We're not talking about an actual job here. This is a volunteer position. There's no pay.

No employees to manage. If anything, it's going to be a pain in the patootie trying to convince certain stiff-necked property owners in this town that they need to make changes." She cast a pointed glance toward Frieda, whose face turned white. "You were eager enough to give Lulu the responsibility of the application. Give her a chance to finish what she started." She sat back in her chair with a thud that tweaked the not-quite-healed muscles surrounding her tailbone. "It's not as if we have volunteers pounding down the doors to take the job."

In the brief silence that followed, Millie congratulated herself. She'd said what needed to be said and defended her friend.

"You make it sound as though we aren't grateful." Frieda swiveled in her chair so that she faced Lulu directly. "You *have* done a tremendous job on the application. Goose Creek is fortunate to have you as a concerned citizen, and we're certainly grateful for your participation on this committee." Then she turned toward Millie. "The fact is, we do have another candidate, one who deserves consideration. Violet Alcorn."

Frieda's words sent a shock of ice water down Millie's spine.

"No." The word came out as a whisper. Millie cleared her throat. "Violet hasn't been involved in this process at all. She doesn't know a thing about the program."

"I've spoken with her at length," Frieda said. "She's read the documentation and is eager to undertake the responsibilities. And since she's lived in Goose Creek for several decades, she has the benefit of having preestablished relationships with the town's leaders and business owners."

"Violet will make a wonderful manager."

Millie aimed a shocked stare at Lulu.

"Really." She held Millie's gaze without blinking. "It's true, what Frieda says. She knows the folks and the town better than me. And whatever she doesn't know, you can help her with, just like you were going to help me. She's your best friend, right?"

To which Millie had no ready reply.

"So we're agreed?" Frieda paused, and when no one voiced an opinion, settled the glasses back on her nose. She picked up a pen and wrote Violet's name on the application. "There. Phyllis, will you make copies and take them to the city council meeting tonight?"

Millie sat numbly while Phyllis took the application. Across the table, Lulu picked up her knitting. Her needles blurred like a hummingbird's wings.

※

Exiting the city hall building, Millie rounded on Lulu. "I can't believe you did that." She tried not to pitch her voice at lecture-tone, but failed. "We had Tuesday on our side, and Phyllis was leaning our way. The three of us could have overridden Frieda, and the job would have been yours."

Lulu adjusted the strap of her knitting bag on her shoulder. "It's the truth, girlie. Violet will be a better manager." She displayed a toothy grimace. "Like my Honey Bun says, sometimes you gotta just take one for the Gipper. Or the Creek."

"I disagree about Violet being better suited for the job." A twinge of disloyalty pinged in the back of Millie's brain, but she ignored it in favor of the truth. "She has many fine qualities, but she's about as organized as a three-year-old. And she can barely spell her own name. You're far better at written communication, and you're…" Millie cast about for a compliment, but the only thing she could think of was the disastrous purple turnip pie. "You're not afraid to experiment with new things. The only thing Violet has going for her that you don't is a friendship with longtime Creekers." She allowed her expression to become stern. "And you *will* have that."

Cocking her head on her long neck, Lulu narrowed her eyes. "You and Violet on the outs, are you?"

"That has nothing to do with it."

"C'mon, girlie." Lulu punched her on the shoulder a little too firmly. "Rocking on a high horse won't get you anything but a sore rump. And you can't afford to do that again, can you?" She indulged in a typical Thacker guffaw, which drew a glance from Hazel Duncan, who was just entering Cardwell's across the street. "Climb down outta that saddle and make up with your friend."

Millie spoke through gritted teeth. "You don't know what you're asking."

The laughter disappeared from Lulu's features. "I have a pretty good idea. You two fell out because of me, and I can't stand the thought."

Sympathy twisted Millie's heart. "It has nothing to do with you," she lied.

Lulu stared at her a moment, eyes narrowed. When she spoke again, it was with a seriousness that Millie had never seen her display.

"Listen, the main reason I wanted that job was so people would look kindly on me. Now is that a good enough reason?" Before Millie could answer, she did. "No. So let Violet have the job. You'll help her, because that's the kind of gal you are. And while you're at it, you might be able to gouge some of the rocks out of the path between my house and hers, if you know what I mean."

Millie knew exactly what she meant.

"Hellloooo!"

They both turned to see Lorna hurrying in their direction at a fast waddle, a large box clutched to her ample bosom. "My dear, you'll never guess what I've found for you."

Since she wasn't close enough to hear, Millie didn't bother to bite back a groan. Another gift? And this after FedEx had delivered a candelabra during breakfast this morning, purchased on eBay.

Millie loaded her voice with all the sternness she could muster. "Lorna, you really must stop buying me gifts. It's embarrassing."

"Nonsense. They're not for you, they're for the B&B." The woman arrived, slightly out of breath, and balanced the box in one hand so she could reach into the purse dangling from her shoulder with the other. "And I got something for you too, my dear. A token in appreciation for chauffeuring me to town." She extracted a bag and offered it to Lulu.

Lulu opened the bag and pulled out a wad of tissue paper.

"Be careful," Lorna cautioned as she unwrapped a pair of small objects.

Displaying her typical tactlessness, Lulu held one of the tiny silver bowls up and asked, "What the heck is that?"

"It's a salt cellar, dear." Lorna poked a finger into the tissue. "And there's a little spoon to go with it. All the best dinner parties have a salt cellar for each guest at their table. I've bought you four, in case you and your husband entertain."

"Well, don't that beat all? My Honey Bun is gonna be so impressed." Lulu displayed a toothy grin. "Thank you, Miss Hinkle. That's awful friendly of you."

"Call me Lorna, dear." She turned a sly smile on Millie. "You must wait to see your gift. I know the perfect place for it. I want you to see it displayed there, so you'll get the full effect."

During the drive home, Lorna prattled on about how much Millie would love the gift she'd purchased, and how beautiful the wedding reception would be, and how hand-thrown pottery bowls could be bought far more cheaply on eBay than at the stores she'd visited that morning. Millie barely listened, her thoughts focused instead on Lulu's comments. Should she take the first step in mending her fences with Violet? Even though the move to steal the manager job from Lulu was a thoroughly despicable act?

They arrived at home, and Lulu parked the car near the porch. When they reached the front door, Lorna stepped in front of them.

"You two wait here," she commanded. "I'll only be a moment."

She entered, closing the door behind her.

"Do you want me to cook something for that reception?" Lulu

asked. "I've got a recipe for mini quiches that look real nice on a fancy doily."

"I don't think that's what Susan has in mind," Millie answered, still distracted by thoughts of Violet. "But thank you for the offer."

The door was thrown wide. Lorna waved an expansive hand. "Enter!"

They stepped inside. At first Millie saw nothing different in the entry hall. Perhaps Lorna's gift had been placed in the parlor.

"Good gravy, would you look at that?"

Lulu had fixed a rather horrified stare on something. Millie followed her gaze. When her eyes fell on the gift, she couldn't hold back a gasp.

There, resting on her Louis XIV entry table, a hideous visage fixed its menacing grimace on her. It was none other than Chester, the appalling clay bust from the Freckled Frog.

# Chapter Fifteen

W hy can't we eat in here like we always do?" Al asked glumly. "You know I don't like putting on airs."

Millie bustled from the refrigerator to the table to pour cream— real cream, he noted—into a small pitcher. "Because it's Sunday, and she's getting up early enough to go to church, and it's the nice thing to do."

"I don't see why I have to be nice. She isn't."

Millie turned a scolding look on him. "Because this is your house, and she is your guest."

"She's a customer," he corrected. "A paying customer." Which, in his opinion, was the only positive thing about Miss High-and-Mighty Hinkle's stay.

"In the B&B business they're called guests." Millie stepped back to examine the coffee tray. "And stop grumbling. You sound like an old bear."

He hadn't realized he'd grumbled, but the remnants of a bearlike growl were rumbling in his chest. Completely justified, in his opinion, but he cut it off in deference to his wife.

At the sound of footsteps on the stairs, Millie glanced upward. "Would you take the coffee tray? I'll get the casserole."

He obeyed and arrived in the dining room at the same time as their guest.

Catching sight of him, she drew up short. Her gaze circled the table. "Three settings this morning?"

Somehow she managed to make the question sound like an insult. Al clamped his jaw tight as Millie entered from the kitchen.

"I thought it would be a nice change to eat family style this morning." Her cheery tone made a pleasant contrast to the Hinkle woman's.

Millie slid the hot casserole onto a trivet in front of his plate. She used her right hand to position the dish. The sling had disappeared several days ago, and though she still wore the wrist brace, she'd assured him the pain was practically gone. Al enjoyed seeing his wife almost back to normal. The sight of her in pain left him feeling helpless and somehow like a failure.

Miss Hinkle gave a haughty sniff. "In all the best B&Bs the owners serve their guests. They don't dine with them."

The words scraped across Al's nerves. "Fine with me." He started to pick up his plate and take it to the kitchen, but Millie stopped him with a tight-lipped glare.

She turned a smile on the odious woman. "I know it's probably not the best practice, but I thought on Sundays we might relax the rules a bit. Since you're staying with us for such a long visit, I've almost come to think of you as family."

Al nearly choked. That old bat, family? Not likely.

The words charmed her though. She reached out a large hand and gave Millie's arm an affectionate pat. "I've grown fond of you too, dear."

She turned an icy glance toward Al, and her lips snapped shut.

What had he done to alienate her? He had no idea. If he could figure it out, he'd do it again in hopes of driving her away.

As he settled the napkin in his lap, he noticed that Millie wore a frozen expression. Miss Hinkle stood beside her chair, looking down her nose at him.

*Oh for heaven's sake.*

Not bothering to hide a sigh, he rose, tossed his napkin on his plate, and slid out her chair.

"Thank you."

He turned to offer his wife the same courtesy. Millie had already seated herself, but she gave an approving nod and a quick wink. That wink did wonders to lighten Al's attitude. They were coconspirators, Millie and he, the same as always. He resettled himself.

"And what is this?" Miss Hinkle fixed a suspicious eye on the food.

"A breakfast casserole. It's one of my specialties." An anxious frown hovered around his wife's lips. "I hope you like it."

At a nod from Millie, Al cut a largish serving and set it in the center of Miss Hinkle's plate.

She inspected the portion. "It isn't very substantial, is it?"

Indignant, Al slapped his own food on his plate. Aware of Millie's anxious presence at the opposite end of the table, he forced a fairly calm reply. "This is a special treat. We usually have banana bran muffins on Sundays."

"Have some fruit," Millie said quickly, passing a bowl filled with a colorful array of fresh fruit.

"No toast?" Miss Hinkle's head moved as she scanned the table. "At these prices, one might at least expect a slice of toast."

"Since there's a crust," Millie said, "I usually forgo other carbs. But if you want toast..."

She half-rose, no doubt preparing to dash for the toaster.

Enough. They might be running a B&B, but Al refused to see his wife turned into a short-order cook. He pointed his fork in her direction, gestured for her to remain seated, and then turned to Miss Hinkle. Adopting the exact tone he used with their grandchildren, he said, "Try it. If you don't like it, we'll get you a bowl of Cheerios."

His affront clear, she picked up her fork and sliced off a miniscule bite. As she chewed, a grudging acceptance crept over her features.

"Very nice." She addressed the compliment toward Millie while cutting a larger chunk. "Though it could use a bit of seasoning. Please pass the salt."

Not at all sure of his ability to maintain his composure, Al finished his breakfast in silence.

❊

When the dishes had been washed and the kitchen cleaned, Al headed for the parlor for a moment's solitude while they waited for Justin and Susan to fetch Miss Hinkle for church. On the way through the entry hall, he felt the itch of a menacing stare. He turned to find the hideous clay head glaring at him from protruding eyeballs. The thing looked like some sort of tribal pagan mask, or perhaps a likeness of Ross Perot. The jack-o'-lantern-like teeth were the stuff of nightmares.

Millie came down the hallway, her hair freshly arranged and her purse swinging from her shoulder.

"Ghastly, isn't it?" she whispered.

"Absolutely," he agreed. "Why haven't you stashed it in a closet somewhere?"

She glanced toward the top of the stairs. "I don't want to be rude."

"Why on earth not?" Al didn't bother to lower his voice. "She doesn't hesitate to be rude."

"Shhh. It was a gift, and even though it isn't our taste, she meant well."

Al gazed at the grim head. "I doubt that. It's hideous, and she bought it to plague me."

"It is horrible." She shuddered and turned her back on it. "I honestly don't want it in the house, not even in a closet. But what can we do? It wouldn't be polite to get rid of it."

An idea flashed into Al's head with startling clarity. If he spent time considering, he'd probably decide against following through with it, but after listening to the sounds of the Shopping Channel drift through the ceiling half the night, and one of the most uncomfortable breakfasts he'd ever eaten, he wasn't feeling particularly polite.

He grasped the head and turned toward the door.

"What are you doing?" Millie's whisper held a touch of urgency.

"Watch."

He swung open the door as Susan's car rolled to a stop at the end of the driveway. Carrying the bust across the porch, he halted at the top of the concrete steps.

"Albert!" Millie ran after him. "Where are you taking it?"

The car doors opened, and Susan and Justin emerged.

A sort of frenzy took possession of Al. The stress of the past week combined and came to rest on the terrible statue that his beloved wife detested but was too nice to get rid of. Well, leave the niceness to Millie. She hated the thing even worse than he, and it was a husband's responsibility to ensure his wife's comfort.

He extended his arms and let the statue slip from his grip. It landed on the edge of the second step, cracked open, and tumbled down the other two. Lumpy ears, eyebrows, and teeth skittered across the walkway.

"Oops," he said with a wide smile.

Millie gasped. Susan froze in her tracks, a wide-eyed stare fixed on the fragments. Justin, on the other hand, let loose with a laugh that rose into the sky. Entirely satisfied, Al dusted his hands together.

The sound of footsteps behind him alerted him to the presence of the gift giver herself. Miss Hinkle appeared in the doorway, handbag slung over one arm.

"There you are, Justin dear. Right on time. I'm ready to—" Her gaze settled on the remnants of Chester littering the steps.

Before she had time to react, Al approached her. "I'm sorry."

The wonder-working words apparently worked only on wives. Miss Hinkle's outraged expression did not fade.

Before she recovered enough to speak, he offered a glib explanation. "I brought it out to examine it more closely in the sunlight, and it slipped right out of my hands." He sidestepped around her. "Excuse me while I get the broom."

Al escaped, leaving Miss Hinkle to sputter on the porch.

❄

Millie emerged from the car in the church parking lot with the shock of Albert's destruction of the horrible sculpture vibrating in her mind.

"I still can't believe it." She eyed him over the rounded top of the pink Volkswagen Beetle. "Whatever possessed you to do such a thing?"

"I've had enough." An easy and entirely unapologetic smile rested on his face. "She's rude and overbearing, and she finds fault with everything. I see no reason we should suffer the presence of one of her unwanted gifts in the entryway of our home."

"She's not that bad, once you get to know her." Whatever the reason behind Albert's actions, it seemed to have done him a world of good. The dark scowl he'd worn for the past week had disappeared, replaced by the pleasant expression she most enjoyed in her stern husband. Perhaps smashing Chester had been a stress-reliever for him.

Al's gaze slid past her and fixed on something behind her head. "Uh, Millie?"

At the sound of Violet's voice, a little stab of sorrow knifed Millie in the chest. She turned to find her former friend standing a short distance away, wringing a tissue in her hands.

"Can we talk?"

In an unusual display of sensitivity, Al said, "I'll see you inside," and slipped away.

"I think we should," Millie answered.

"I've wanted to call you all week to say…" Her features scrunched, and bursting into tears, she buried her face in the tissue.

The pain in her heart dissolved, and Millie rushed forward to gather her best friend in an embrace. Tears filled her own eyes as she hugged with all her strength. "I've been so miserable without you."

"Me too." Her body shook with sobs. "I'm sorry, I really am."

"I'm sorry too," Millie managed between blubbers. "I know how

Lulu gets on your nerves, and I tried to force the two of you together anyway."

Violet shook her head. "It's my fault. I was just plain eaten up with jealousy. I somehow got in my head if you started liking her, you wouldn't like me anymore."

"I *love* you, Violet. You're my best friend. Nothing can ever change that."

They stood for a long moment, hugging and crying, while cars parked around them and curious people streamed past. Millie didn't care, not even when Sally Bright stared with such fixed attention she walked into a parked car.

When their tears slowed, Violet pulled back. "I'm sorry about the manager job too. I called Frieda yesterday and told her to take my name off, but she said the application had already been filed."

"Whatever made you say you'd do it in the first place?"

Violet dabbed at her eyes with the shreds of her tissue. "Spite at first. But then I started reading up on the program and I realized what a good thing it will be for Goose Creek. The longer I thought about it, the more ideas I came up with for dressing up Main Street." She gave a tiny laugh. "You know how much time I have on my hands."

A touch of longing hovered in the watery eyes. Surprised, Millie shifted mental gears. She'd assumed Violet had volunteered as a slap at Lulu, or perhaps under pressure from Frieda. The idea that she might actually *want* the job had never entered Millie's mind.

But why not? Violet was a few years younger than Millie. She'd been able to retire from her government job early, in part because she'd gone to work directly after high school and so had reached her thirty-year anniversary in her late forties. Also because her husband's death had left her with a small income. She had no children, no close relatives, and years ahead of her. Millie's postretirement goal was not to kick back and settle into a dormant life, but to open a B&B. Why shouldn't Violet have a similar goal?

"Do you *want* the job?" she asked.

The answer was a hesitant shrug. "It would be fun." Then she straightened. "But I won't take it. Since the application's already filed, I'll wait until it's approved by the state, and then I'll resign so Lulu can have it."

Thoughts whirling, Millie pulled her into another hug. Two friends, one job. And her in the middle. While she could easily envision Lulu assisting Violet, it would take a lot of persuasion and diplomacy to convince Violet to assist Lulu. Either way, every time the two clashed, Millie would be dragged into the conflict.

If there was a solution to be found, it would take thought and patience. Right now she didn't have the energy for either.

With a final hug, she released Violet. "Come on. Let's go to the ladies' room and fix our makeup before church starts."

An unsolved problem still hovered, but it was with a light heart that Millie entered the church arm in arm with her best friend.

❊

"Glad to see you two made up," Al said as he turned from the parking lot onto Walnut Street.

Millie twisted around to bestow a smile on Violet. "We are too."

"You can't get rid of me, Al," Violet teased, sounding like her old self. "I'm stuck to Millie like gum on the bottom of her shoe."

Millie laughed. "Except I like you, and I'm not fond of gum on my shoe."

Violet cocked her head. "How about this? We go together like peas and carrots."

Albert kept his eyes on the road. "What does that make me?"

"Onions," Violet answered without an instant's hesitation. "The small cocktail onions that dress up a dish of peas and carrots."

They laughed, and Millie marveled at her husband joining in the lighthearted banter. Smashing Chester had worked wonders on his mood. As for her, she looked forward to the return of the Sunday afternoon tradition of leftovers for lunch with her husband and her friend. The remains of last night's chicken would easily feed three, and she had the fixings for a salad.

When he turned onto the long driveway leading to their home, Albert put a foot on the break. "Whose car is that?"

Millie peered through the windshield at a blue vehicle parked in the circle. "I've never seen it before."

"Looks like it's been ridden hard and put away wet," Violet commented.

Cliché, perhaps, but appropriate in this case. The car had been neglected and bore signs of several fender benders that were never repaired. Paint bubbled on the hood, and a crack spidered across the windshield.

Albert inclined his head. "The driver doesn't look much better."

Until then Millie had not spotted the young man sitting on the top porch step. His windblown hair hung long and loose to his shoulders, and the knees of his jeans were threadbare. He sat with his arms dangling between long legs, shoulders drooping, and a solemn expression on his face. When Albert parked the car behind his, he hefted himself off the step slowly, as though his body weighed a ton. Not true, since his clothing hung loosely from a slight frame.

"Stay in the car," Albert commanded.

Millie shot a surprised glance at him, but he'd already opened the door to exit.

"He thinks we need protection." Violet ducked her head to peer through the glass. "Though I don't think that one means any mischief."

"Not at all." Millie studied him as Albert approached, his words not discernible. "The poor thing looks sad, not violent."

The two men shook hands, though no smile appeared on the stranger's face. He said something and shoved his hand in his pocket. Albert whirled, eyebrows puckered, and waved impatiently for her to join him. She and Violet exited the car. What in the world had the young man said to provoke her husband from his good mood?

He spoke in a tight voice. "Millie, this is Ross Mayfield." She extended a hand to take his but froze when Albert continued. "He's Justin's cousin, here for the wedding."

The young man shook her hand, his grasp slack. "I thought you knew I was coming, but apparently not."

"Of course we expected you," Millie rushed to say. "Only perhaps not quite this soon."

He nodded, and if possible his shoulders slumped even further. "I didn't have anything else going on, and Aunt Lorna said it would be okay." A resigned sigh escaped his lips. "Don't worry. I'll go home."

"Where is home?"

"New York."

"Goodness, that's a long drive." Millie avoided looking at the car. If the engine were in a similar state as the exterior, it was a miracle he'd made it.

"Not many people your age can take off work for two weeks." Albert had not lost his suspicious expression. "What do you do for a living, Mayfield?"

Hands in his pockets, he shrugged. "I'm a writer."

"Oh, how exciting." Millie found herself smiling with far more enthusiasm than normal, as if some of her energy might spill over onto the poor man. "What do you write?"

"Blogs."

A moment's silence descended while Millie struggled for an appropriate response.

"I know. Unimpressive, right?" Ross kicked mournfully at the grass. "I used to write for magazines, but the work dried up. Now I write blogs." He slouched toward his car. "Is it okay if I come back a couple of days early? I haven't seen my cousin in a while, and I figured we could catch up. Not that he's likely to want to. Nothing much about my life worth telling."

What a pitiful young man. She'd never seen anyone as down-hearted. Millie cast a desperate glance at Albert and included a silent plea.

Lifting his eyes toward the sky, Albert hesitated before giving a grudging nod.

"Wait!" Millie caught Ross by the arm and noted in passing that he could use a few good meals to put some meat on those bones. "I'd hate for you to make that drive twice, especially when we have plenty of room. And I'm sure Justin and Susan will be delighted you're here. Please stay."

Relief glimmered in his eyes. "If you're sure I won't be in the way."

"Of course not. I look forward to getting to know you better." She waved Violet over. "I'd like you to meet my friend, Violet Alcorn. Violet, this is Mr. Mayfield."

"The name's Ross." He treated Violet to the same quick handshake.

"And I'm Millie. You've already met my husband."

Albert drew himself up to eye the young man. "You've been informed of our rates, I assume?"

Heat burned in Millie's cheeks. Must he bring up money within minutes of meeting the man?

On second thought, Albert was right. They were running a B&B—or were *practicing* to run a B&B—and must treat every transaction as business.

To her alarm, the young man shook his head. "I haven't a cent. See?" He turned out his pockets to reveal nothing but a set of car keys. "Aunt Lorna is picking up the tab. She insisted. That's the only way I could afford to come."

"That will be fine," Millie hurried to say before Albert could object. "Why don't you get your luggage, and I'll show you upstairs. You'll be staying in the room Justin occupied while he lived with us. We call it the Little Boy Blue room."

While he went to the trunk of his car, Violet edged close.

"Appropriate to put him in that room," she whispered.

Millie glanced at her. "Why do you say that?"

"He's the bluest boy I've ever seen. I wonder why he's got such a long face."

"I don't know," Millie said. "But I'm sure I'll find out."

# Breakfast Casserole

1 can crescent rolls
8 oz. ham, cubed
8 oz. shredded sharp cheddar cheese
½ medium onion, diced
½ green bell pepper, diced
1 T. olive oil
8 eggs
16 oz. (1 pint) half-and-half

Spread crescent rolls in bottom of 9 x 13 pan and press the edges together to form a crust. Sauté the onion and pepper in olive oil until soft and the onion is translucent. Remove from heat and stir in the ham. Spread that mixture evenly over the crust. Next layer on the cheese. In a medium bowl, whisk the eggs and half-and-half, and pour that over the cheese. Cover and refrigerate overnight.

In the morning, set the casserole out for 15 minutes. Uncover and bake in an oven preheated to 350 for 45 minutes. Remove from the oven and let the casserole rest for 15 minutes before serving.

# Chapter Sixteen

Hold her really still. This isn't going to hurt, but it might startle her."

Serious-faced, the little girl grasped the white bunny on the exam table.

With a thumb and finger, Susan forced the rabbit's mouth open. Moving quickly, she positioned the clippers around the overgrown front teeth and applied a firm squeeze. An audible snap sounded, and both the bunny and the child jumped.

"There. All done." She smiled at the child.

Tears filled Missy's eyes as she cuddled her pet. "You're sure that didn't hurt Snowy?"

"Not at all," Susan promised. "That stuff I rubbed on her gums numbed them completely."

Mrs. Ingersoll, who had been sitting in the corner chair, rose and put an arm around her daughter's shoulders. "How often will we have to do this?"

"It's hard to tell." Susan set the clippers on the counter and made a notation on Snowy's chart. "I'm pretty sure the malocclusion is only affecting the front teeth, which is good. You need to make sure she has chew toys, especially wooden ones. They'll help keep the teeth worn down. But I expect you'll have to bring her in here every couple of months, if not sooner."

"How long till she gets better?" Missy asked.

"Snowy's not sick, sweetie. Her teeth just don't line up right." Susan shook her head. "They'll always be like that."

She opened the door, and Missy exited. Mrs. Ingersoll followed more slowly and stopped to whisper in Susan's ear. "That was the worst Easter present ever. I never thought I'd be paying for orthodontic care for a rabbit."

"We can work out a frequent patient discount," Susan promised.

In the waiting room she was pleased to see that the Wainright boys had packed up their toys and were each absorbed in an electronic game. They'd been here for close to an hour while Fern went for another interview, this time for an after-school babysitting job.

When Alice asked if the boys could come, Susan wanted to say no. She couldn't be sure they'd been responsible for the altercation between the beagle and the Siamese cat, but the discovery of dog treats in the cat room not an hour after they'd left the last time was certainly suspicious. Thank goodness she'd found the catnip-filled ball in the dog waiting room before further damage was done. But today, at least, the boys were on their best behavior.

While Alice ran Mrs. Ingersoll's credit card, a familiar figure entered the clinic. Susan swallowed back a groan and greeted Aunt Lorna with a hug.

"What a nice surprise. I wasn't expecting to see you until dinner." She greeted Ross, who slumped in behind his aunt, with a forced smile.

The nightly dinners with Justin's aunt, and now his doleful cousin, were beginning to wear on her. A few times she'd scraped up a plausible excuse to miss, but she felt guilty leaving Justin to deal with his relatives alone. And since Aunt Lorna didn't drive, they couldn't very well leave her with Millie and Al every night. Millie would have readily agreed to feed her guest dinner, but a B&B was supposed to provide breakfast, not three meals a day.

"It's been a treat having dear Ross to chauffer me around." She patted Ross's shoulder. "I've been able to see some of the countryside in the daylight."

A ray of hope brightened Susan's thoughts. Maybe now that Ross had arrived, he could take dinner duty every so often and let Susan and Justin enjoy some time alone.

"Have you visited Kentucky before?" she asked him.

"No," came the dispirited answer.

Susan gritted her teeth. Justin and she had discussed his cousin on the way home last night. That Ross was depressed was obvious and even understandable given his lack of a steady job. But Justin said he'd been gloomy even as a boy.

"You're here at a beautiful time of year." She smiled broadly, hoping he might return the gesture. "Be sure to drive out to the Kentucky Horse Park. It's not too far, and really worth a visit."

Aunt Lorna took her by the arm. "I wanted to talk to you about something. Is there someplace we can speak privately?"

At the idea of being closeted with Aunt Lorna in her tiny office, a panicky tickle erupted in Susan's stomach. She might never escape. Far better to stay where she could rely on interruptions, such as the arrival of her next patient in—she glanced at her watch—less than ten minutes.

"Um, I don't have much time. How about if we sit here?" She pointed to the Playful Pups room, which was vacant.

Aunt Lorna allowed herself to be guided to a seat and patted the one next to her. Ross slumped in a chair in the corner and began leafing through a copy of *Modern Dog*.

"About the pastor's office," Aunt Lorna began, and Susan swallowed a groan. "Please tell me why you decided on that location instead of the sanctuary." She leaned forward and held Susan's gaze. "Are you an atheist?"

Susan shook her head. "We didn't see the sense in using the sanctuary since we aren't having an actual wedding ceremony with music and guests and all that."

A pained look settled on Aunt Lorna's face. "Explain to me again why we're not having guests."

They'd gone over this a dozen times, but Susan exercised patience and repeated the explanation. "I've only lived in Goose Creek two years, and I spend all my time here at the clinic. My friends are mostly animals. Most of the people I know are pet owners. If I begin inviting clients, I'll have to invite them all, or someone's sure to feel left out. Before I know it, we'd end up inviting half the town. Neither Justin nor I are fond of big parties, so we want to celebrate our marriage privately." She smiled. "With the people we truly love. Our family."

There. Maybe flattery would work.

"That is very touching, my dear." Aunt Lorna picked up Susan's hand and held it, patting it with her other. "I have a suggestion I'd like you to consider, but I don't want you to think I'm trying to meddle."

A laugh almost escaped. Only with firm self-control was Susan able to keep a straight face. "What do you suggest?"

"What if we held the ceremony at the Richardsons' B&B?" She lifted a finger to forestall a quick answer. "Not a big wedding, merely the simple ceremony you and Justin have your hearts set on. A straightforward exchange of vows."

Amazed that Justin's prediction had come true so soon, Susan opened her mouth to deliver a firm *no*.

Aunt Lorna waved a hand. "Before you answer, allow me to point out a few things you may not have considered. First, there's the matter of your guests' comfort."

"The pastor's office isn't uncomfortable. There's even a small sofa."

"I'm sure it's quite cozy, but it can't possibly be as comfortable or as beautiful as Millie's parlor. Or the backyard, with that gazebo, and the sunlight filtering through the trees, and the flowers blooming all around."

The image she painted rose in vivid detail in Susan's imagination. The B&B's grounds were full of charm. While Justin lived there, Susan had spent enough time cuddled with him in that gazebo to develop a sentimental attachment to it.

She shook herself. "I couldn't possibly impose on Millie and Al any more than I already have."

"Susan dear, you know they wouldn't mind. It's obvious to anyone with eyes that they're fond of you and Justin. Otherwise they wouldn't have offered to host the reception. And then there's the matter of convenience."

"Convenience?"

"Perhaps it has escaped your notice, but every one of your guests will already be at the B&B. Instead of asking us to pile into cars, drive across town to stand in a cramped office for a ten-minute ceremony, and then drive back for the reception, think how much easier it will be to walk downstairs."

Susan had no ready reply. With the logistics laid out like that, Aunt Lorna's suggestion made perfect sense.

"Oh!" The woman held her hand in front of her mouth, eyes round. "I've just realized the reason you might not want to do that. How stupid of me."

"What reason is that?"

"If you get married at the B&B, of course the Richardsons will be present. Excluding them would be inexcusably rude." She leaned forward. "Not wanting them at your wedding is understandable. Millie is, after all, your employee."

A hot flush stole up Susan's neck. She glanced at Alice, who couldn't help but overhear the conversation in the small reception area. Alice was bent over a patient's chart, scribbling with a pencil.

"That's not it at all," Susan insisted. "We love Millie and Al. They've become like family to both of us." She wanted to add, *Much closer than some family members.*

"Then holding the wedding at their house will give you the perfect excuse to include them without the worry of offending others." The smile on her face held a note of triumph. "I think it's an idea worth considering."

Susan sat back in her chair, chagrined at the realization that she'd been manipulated again. But this change made so much sense. Never mind the fact that Millie's house was beautiful, thanks in part to Justin's handyman work on the renovations.

"Well." Aunt Lorna rocked forward and stood. "You think about it. Discuss it with Justin, and let me know what you decide. Ross, would you mind driving me to that little town we passed through this morning? I glimpsed a quaint little tea shop I'd like to visit."

"Might as well." He unfolded his lanky frame. "I don't have anything else to do."

Susan walked to the door, her stomach churning with discomfort. What would Justin say when she told him she wanted to get married at Millie's B&B? Probably that she'd just taken another step down that slippery slope.

But this was as far as she would go. From now on, Aunt Lorna's suggestions would be answered with a firm *no*. Of course, there couldn't be much more she'd want to change. Only one that Susan could think of.

She paused with her hand on the doorknob and looked the formidable lady directly in the eye. "Before you get any other ideas, I want to say that I will not wear a wedding gown. I already have my dress, and Justin is going to wear his suit."

Disappointment flooded Aunt Lorna's eyes, which let Susan know she'd hit the nail on the head.

"What color is your dress?" she asked.

"Creamy white and tea length. It's bridal enough to be suitable, but I'll be able to wear it to dinner, or to church, or anywhere."

The large nostrils flared. "It sounds very functional."

The description gave Susan pause. Was that an insult or a compliment?

"Thank you," she said, deciding on the latter.

When the pair had exited, Susan turned to Alice. "You are more than welcome to come to my wedding. I'd love to have you there."

Grinning, Alice shook her head. "Thank you, but no. My feelings aren't hurt at all, so don't give it another thought."

Forest piped up from the Kuddly Kitties area. "Can I come?"

Relieved that Alice wasn't offended, Susan turned toward the boys. "Sorry. Adults only."

"Oh, man!" He slumped in his chair. "Grown-ups have all the fun."

*Not true,* she wanted to say. Playing computer games and drawing pictures sounded a lot more fun than nightly dinners with Aunt Lorna and gloomy Cousin Ross. Instead, she headed for the back to get Exam Room One ready for her next patient.

※

For nearly a decade, Millie and Violet had enjoyed a ritual tea on Thursday afternoons. Last week had been the first time they'd missed, except for vacations and holidays. Millie planned this one with extra care, viewing it as a celebration of their renewed friendship.

"You've gone all out," Violet exclaimed upon entering the dining room and spying the linen napkins and the crystal dishes on the three-tiered serving tray. "I feel like the Queen of England."

"We never used the dining room until Lorna arrived." Millie indicated where Violet should sit. "And I was thinking what a shame that is. High tea should be taken in elegant surroundings, don't you think?"

"You took the words right out of my mouth." Violet sat and eyed the treats. "You made my favorite mini scones and fake Devonshire cream. Thank you."

"Of course." Millie removed the tea cozy and tapped a finger on the side of the china pot to test the temperature before filling Violet's cup and then her own.

"I don't remember that tray. Is it new?"

Millie followed Violet's gaze to the silver serving tray on the sideboard. "It's a gift from Lorna. She gave me the matching chafing dish too."

"Looks expensive. Is that real silver?"

"Oh, I'm sure it's just silver plated." Millie set her teacup in the saucer. "Honestly, she gives me so many gifts, it's embarrassing."

Violet put two scones and three cucumber sandwiches on her plate. "The reason's clear as a bell. She's trying to curry favor."

"That must be it, though I hate to think anyone would feel the need to buy my cooperation."

Violet paused in the act of serving herself a spoonful of chocolate-covered almonds. "What does she want you to cooperate with?"

"The wedding." Selecting a scone, Millie shook her head. "I've told her I'm thrilled Susan agreed to have the ceremony and the reception here. But apparently Lorna feels like she has to bribe me into agreeing. And it's not just me. You should see all the stuff she's bought for Susan and Justin."

Violet slurped from her cup and then set it back in the saucer. "Maybe she's insecure and feels like she has to buy people's affection."

"Possibly, but I think there's more to it than that." Millie glanced toward the doorway that led to the entry hall. Lorna and Ross had left several hours ago for another driving tour of the area. "Come with me. I want to show you something."

They left their tea on the table, and Millie led Violet upstairs.

"Every day she gets new deliveries. Wedding gifts, she says. I've seen more of the FedEx man this week than I have of Albert."

At the top of the stairs, she approached the Bo Peep room on tiptoes, which was silly since she knew no one was inside. Still, she was probably violating some sort of ethics code by showing a guest's room to a friend. But Violet could be trusted.

"Every day when I come in here to make up her bed, it looks worse." She twisted the antique crystal doorknob and threw the door open.

The beautiful soft shell pink paint they'd selected for the walls could barely be glimpsed behind the boxes stacked nearly to the ceiling. The armchair Lorna had purchased sat in the center of the room, squarely in front of the television Justin had installed on the chest of drawers, surrounded by cartons. Lorna had obviously been using one large box as a TV tray, for the cardboard surface bore cookie crumbs and ring-shaped stains as though from a glass or mug. The beautiful area rug she'd purchased was visible only in a wide path that led from the bed to the bathroom.

Violet gasped. "Good gracious, the woman's a hoarder."

"I think she must be." Millie shook her head. "Or maybe she's just addicted to shopping. Every time a new delivery arrives, she says it's another gift for the happy couple. Or for me. Or today, for Ross."

The rumble of a muffler in need of repair drifted in through an open window at the other end of the hallway. That could only be Ross's car.

"It's them!"

Millie slammed the door shut and followed Violet down the stairs at a trot. They dashed into the dining room. By the time the front door opened, they were both seated at the table, sipping their tea with pinkies extended.

When Lorna spied them her eyes lit. "I'd no idea you indulged in the habit of afternoon tea."

Millie displayed a calm smile that did not betray her pounding heart. "Would you like to join us?"

"I would love to."

While she selected a seat, Millie rose to fetch another teacup and plate from the sideboard. "Ross, would you like some tea?"

The young man replied with his habitual gloom. "I guess not. I'd better get upstairs and do some work."

"What are you writing about?" Violet asked.

"Goose Creek." The answer came in a despondent tone. "Might as well, since I'm here."

Millie awarded the young man a bright smile. "I'd like to read it."

"That would be nice." A sigh escaped. "At least I'd know some-body's reading my blog."

He slumped away, the sound of his footsteps heavy on the stairs.

Millie faced Lorna across the table. "I'm worried about that young man."

"Never met such an Eeyore," Violet agreed.

"He's fine." Lorna waved a hand in Ross's direction. "All he needs is one success, and he'll hit his stride." She examined the treats on the tiered rack with sparkling eyes. "Now, what do we have here?"

❄

Shortly after noon on Friday, another package arrived addressed to Millie Richardson.

"This one was overnighted," the FedEx man said as Millie signed his electronic gadget. "Must be something important."

She handed the device back to him. "How's your wife's wasp sting?"

"Much better this morning." The man smiled. "She said to tell you thanks for the tip about the tea bag."

Holding the box, Millie watched him return to his truck. Honestly, she'd miss him when Lorna left. Any man who spoke so often of his wife and children was high on her list.

Inside, she carried the box into the parlor. With a decorative letter opener she sliced the tape and folded back the flaps to reveal several bubble-wrapped items inside. She'd just lifted the first one out when Lorna entered the room.

"I thought I heard the bell. Oh, good." She nodded toward the box. "The package arrived. I can't wait to see it. So often the online photos misrepresent the actual item, you know."

Millie unwrapped several layers of plastic and then gasped as she uncovered a shining silver teapot. "Oh my!"

Lorna smiled widely. "Ah, yes. Exactly how it looked online. It's lovely, don't you think?"

"It's beautiful." Millie examined the intricate design. She'd never seen anything quite so exquisite.

"The scrolling is repousse, late-nineteenth century. There should be a matching sugar bowl and cream pitcher in the box as well."

Millie folded the bubble wrap back over the piece and returned it to the box. She turned to face her guest. "I can't accept this. It's far too expensive a gift."

"Truly, it wasn't," Lorna assured her. "I'm an expert at finding quality items at drastically reduced prices."

Millie narrowed her eyes to study the woman. "How much is *drastically reduced*?"

Shaking her head, Lorna *tsk*ed. "I thought you had better manners than to ask the price of a gift. Trust me. You'd be shocked at the bargain I struck. Besides, I think it would be nice to have tea at the reception, don't you?"

"That would be good, as long as Sus—"

"Susan won't care." She waved a hand in the air. "She's left the menu up to us, so if we want to serve tea, we shall. But really, Millie dear, yesterday's high tea was so delightful I want to encourage you to continue the practice. Your future guests deserve to be treated with elegance, don't you think?"

"Of course, but—"

"Then I won't hear another word on the subject."

She swept from the room, leaving Millie holding the most beautiful teapot she'd ever seen.

## Kentucky-Style Devonshire Cream

4 oz. cream cheese, softened
1 tsp. sugar
1 cup cold whipping cream

Combine cream cheese and sugar until the sugar is completely incorporated. Pour in the whipping cream and stir to blend. Using an electric mixer, beat until fluffy and stiff. Cover and refrigerate until thoroughly chilled.

In England, Devonshire cream is typically served with scones at teatime. To host a traditional Cream Tea, spread a thick layer of Devonshire cream on a sliced scone and top with a spoonful of jam, such as strawberry or blackberry. Devonshire cream can also be spread on bagels or butter cookies and makes a rich and tasty dip for fresh strawberries.

# Chapter Seventeen

Standing on the veranda holding his fourth cup of coffee—decaf, at Millie's insistence—Al listened to his wife recite the list of chores he was to accomplish before she returned from shopping.

"And the railing is loose on the far side." Millie pointed toward the gazebo. "I noticed it yesterday. Would you tighten it up?"

"Tighten the railing," he repeated. "Got it."

She turned her attention to the path leading away from the veranda. "One of those pavers wobbled yesterday when I stepped on it. I think it's uneven or something. I'd hate for Susan to trip on her way to the gazebo."

"I thought they were getting married in the parlor."

"Only if it rains." Millie's glance circled the yard. "If the weather's nice, Lorna thinks it will be beautiful out here."

Since this part of the yard was where Al had spent most of his efforts, he felt a bit flattered. "Consider the path leveled."

Her gaze rose to the woodwork above his head. "The paint on those beams is beginning to flake."

He drew himself up. "That's where I draw the line. I'm already wasting a vacation day on household chores. I refuse to spend my Friday off painting ceiling beams that no one will notice."

Dimples appeared in Millie's cheeks. "I just wanted to see how far I could push before you balked."

Al caught her around the waist with his free arm. "You're a wicked woman, Mildred Richardson."

Giggling, she brushed a quick kiss on his lips. He was about to return the gesture when the door opened behind him.

"Oh!" Miss Hinkle leveled a stern look on them. "There are certain things a guest doesn't expect to encounter."

Speaking of wicked women.

Millie stepped back, and Al let her go reluctantly and tried not to scowl. Private moments with Millie had become too infrequent since the Hinkle woman's arrival.

Violet's car pulled into the driveway.

"There's our ride." Millie retrieved her purse from the patio table. Though she was able to use her injured wrist more and more each day, driving her car with the stick shift still put too much strain on it. Thank goodness she'd made up with Violet, or Al might have found himself playing chauffeur to Miss Hinkle and Millie.

"Is Ross coming shopping with us?" Millie asked Miss Hinkle.

"He's busy working on his blog. Have you got our list?"

Millie pulled a sheet of paper from her purse, covered front and back with handwriting, and held it aloft.

Al eyed the note skeptically. "That's a pretty long list. Didn't Susan and Justin say they only wanted sandwiches and a cake?"

"We're keeping it simple," Millie assured him.

"Don't go overboard," he called after them as they headed for Violet's car. "The wedding's still a week away, and our freezer's already full."

Miss Hinkle turned, eyes bright. "Oh, do you need a new freezer?"

Millie practically shouted, "No!"

Then she blew a kiss in his direction, and they climbed into Violet's car.

❈

Not long after they left, a car engine coming up the driveway interrupted Al's work on the gazebo railing. Surprised, he looked up and watched for the vehicle to come into view around the house. They certainly hadn't been gone long. He wasn't expecting them to return for another couple of hours.

The car that rolled to a stop at the end of the driveway was not Violet's Ford. A fifty-something man emerged and, shielding his eyes with a hand, studied the house intently. A frown gathered on his broad forehead. What was he scowling at? Al looked at the roof. Was there a squirrel up there, preparing to wreak destruction on the wood trim again? If so, he couldn't see it.

"Hello," he called.

Alerted to his presence, the man ceased his inspection of the roof and approached. He wore a suit and tie—an uncommon sight in Goose Creek, where even the mayor dressed casually. He crossed the lawn, his gaze scanning the veranda.

Al set down his hammer and extended a hand. "I'm Al Richardson."

"Mark Logan. I'm here to see Mrs. Richardson."

"She's not here. Was she expecting you?"

Tight lips moved in what might have been taken for a smile. "Yes, but probably not this soon."

Mark. Wait a minute. Wasn't that was the name of Susan's uncle, her father's buddy? For crying out loud, couldn't any of Millie's guests show up on time? The wedding was still eight days away.

Al was about to deliver a biting comment about reservations and the importance of keeping to a planned schedule, but Millie would be furious with him if he turned away one of her practice guests. He'd already endured a scolding for grilling Mayfield about the money. She'd extracted a promise that he was more than happy to make—leave the business of running the B&B to her.

Resigned to his role of maintenance man, Al told Uncle Mark, "I don't expect her for an hour or so, but I can show you upstairs."

He blinked, and his gaze again rose to the roof. "That'll be fine."

Al led him inside through the kitchen door, which would probably give Millie fits. She'd want her guest to see the grand entry hall first, but Al saw no sense in tromping all the way around the house to go in the front door with a more direct route a few yards away. Mark followed quietly behind. Not much of a talker, this fellow. Al approved. A backward glance as they entered the dining room revealed that Mark's sharp eye was taking in every detail, from the molding to the chandelier. He even paused once to test an ancient floorboard with his foot.

"My wife insists on leaving the old wood," Al commented. "It'll have to be resurfaced sometime. I think those vinyl strips that look like wood would wear better and be cheaper in the long run."

Mark jerked his gaze to Al's face, eyes widened with what looked like shock. "This floor is over a hundred years old."

"My point exactly. Out with the old, in with the new, that's my motto. But the wife disagrees, and since it's still solid, there's no reason to spend the money."

Judging by the frown gathered on the man's forehead, he was a purist like Millie. Fine. Let Millie give him the grand tour when she returned. She was better at talking to people anyway. He'd stick with his honey-do list.

Upstairs, he led the man to one of the middle rooms, the only renovated one left unoccupied.

"What's in there?" Mark asked, pointing to the door of one of the turret rooms.

"A bunch of old stuff. My wife hasn't remodeled that one yet, but I think she's planning on calling it the Old King Cole room and making it like a palace." He opened the door where Mark would be staying. "You're in the Humpty Dumpty room."

The man came to a halt on the worn carpet, his expression perplexed. "I am?"

"Don't worry," Al said. "It's not covered in smashed eggshells or anything. But there is a picture of Humpty Dumpty on the wall."

Wearing a dazed look, Mark entered, his neck craning to take in every aspect of the bedroom. Actually, this was Al's favorite because it was the plainest of the three Millie and Violet had decorated. White walls—the paint was called eggshell, Millie told him, hence the room's designation—and wood trim with a nice quilt on the bed.

Best get one thing out of the way right up front. "We do have wireless, but there's no television in this room."

Mark blinked but did not flinch, which Al took as a positive sign. At least Millie wouldn't feel the need to run out and buy another TV.

They stood for a moment in an awkward silence. Should he offer help with the luggage? No, the man looked able-bodied, and Al was not a porter. Let him carry his own suitcase.

He edged toward the door. "When my wife gets home I'll let her know you're here. I'm sure she'll come up and tell you about breakfast times and all."

"I'll, uh, probably take a drive. Look around town a bit."

"Not much to see in Goose Creek." Al gave a companionable laugh. "Not unless you like old buildings."

For the first time, Mark displayed a flicker of interest. "Actually, I do."

"Then be sure to stop in Cardwell Drugstore. Leonard Cardwell's done a bang-up job on the place. If you're hungry, the soda counter's got the best apple pie in three counties." He started to leave but then remembered. This was Susan's uncle, or something like that. "You'll probably want to stop by the Veterinary Clinic and say hi to Dr. Susan. Her place is on Tolouse Street, one street west of Main. Can't miss it."

Receiving only a jerked nod as an answer, Al left and closed the door behind him. Odd fellow, that one. Not much of a talker. A bit slow on the uptake too.

With a shrug, he descended the stairs and returned to his chores.

❋

Millie slumped in the passenger seat while Violet executed a turn onto Main Street. Shopping with Lorna had about done her in. Though Millie usually enjoyed shopping, trying to rein in Lorna's penchant for extravagance had felt like attempting to harness a wild horse. And they'd only been after groceries. Her body felt like someone had hung bricks from her shoulders, and she'd almost drifted off to sleep several times on the forty-minute drive from Lexington to Goose Creek.

"Violet dear, could we stop by the Freckled Frog?" Planted in the center of the backseat, Lorna leaned forward to position her head between Millie's and Violet's shoulders. "I want to see if a replacement can be made for the bust that fell victim to Mr. Richardson's clumsy fingers."

Millie jerked upright. "No, it can't. Frieda told me it was one of a kind."

"Perhaps I could commission one to be made."

Thoughts whirling, Millie exchanged a quick glance with Violet. "I appreciate the offer, Lorna, I really do. But I must insist. You've been far too generous already. I'd feel too guilty to enjoy the gift."

"Well." She leaned back, clearly disappointed. "I wanted to take another look at a hat I saw in there. I'm not sure about the color, but I think it would go well with the dress I plan to wear to the wedding."

Millie sagged against the seatback. She absolutely could not walk through another store.

Violet apparently felt the same. "I'll be glad to stop so you can run inside. Better be quick, though, or that shrimp's going to thaw."

"Quite right. Just pull over there, dear." A large finger pointed to the empty parking place in front of the Frog. Lorna climbed out and before she closed the door told them, "I'll be back before you know I've gone."

"Quick as a flash." Violet awarded Millie a grin as the door slammed shut. She adored finding an appropriate situation for a cliché.

"I'm so tired." Millie leaned her head against the window, eyes drifting closed. "I hope Albert doesn't mind ham sandwiches and chips for supper. That's about all I can manage tonight."

"That is the spendingest woman I've ever seen." Violet shook her head. "I thought for sure she was going to talk you into the caviar."

"And the standing rib roast." Millie yawned. "If I let her get away with a six-course meal, like she wants, Susan will fire me for sure."

The car went silent, and tiredness buzzed along Millie's limbs. If Lorna didn't hurry, she'd fall asleep for sure.

"Who do you suppose that is?" Violet asked.

Millie opened her eyes to find her friend pointing through the windshield at a man walking down the other side of the street, his gait slow. A nice-looking gentleman in his suit and short-cropped hair. He stopped in front of Randy Offutt's vacant building and, bending to examine the windowsill, jotted a note on a tablet. While they watched, he extracted a cell phone, snapped a picture of the sill, and then stepped back to take one of the entire storefront.

"Maybe he's thinking of buying Randy's building?"

"That's exciting. I wonder what kind of store he'd put in there."

The man turned and aimed his cell phone down the line of buildings toward Tuesday's Day Spa before continuing on his way. He disappeared inside Cardwell Drugstore.

The back door opened, and Lorna slid into the car. "See? I told you I wouldn't be long." She settled a large bag in the seat beside her and then closed the door.

"Did the hat match?" Millie asked.

"Perfectly. Take a look."

She extracted a hat box and opened the lid. Millie and Violet peered inside. Frieda had found a buyer for her three-hundred-dollar Derby hat.

※

By the time Al finished cleaning his teeth and climbed into bed, Millie was already asleep. The magazine she'd been reading lay open on her chest, and her head leaned back against the headboard, eyes closed. He stood beside the bed, gazing down at her. Though there was no evidence of her dimples, he fought an urge to lean over and kiss her still-smooth cheek.

She spoke without opening her eyes. "You're staring at me. I can feel it."

"Because you're beautiful."

He gave in to the impulse and stooped to kiss her. The dimple appeared where his lips had touched. She put an arm around his neck and drew him close for a proper kiss.

"Thank you for working so hard today. And especially for painting that crossbeam on the veranda. It looks much better."

When he straightened, she folded her magazine and set it on her nightstand. He slid into bed and scooted to the center, where she nestled at his side, resting her head in the indentation of his shoulder. A perfect fit.

"The whole thing does need to be painted," he admitted, "but I didn't have time."

"It can wait until summer." A yawn ended the comment.

Footsteps creaked overhead, followed by the sound of something being dragged across the floor.

Al glared upward. "What on earth is the woman doing?"

"Probably rearranging all those boxes so she can see the television better," Millie answered, her words heavy with sleep.

"Well, at least your new guest is quiet."

"Ross? I've barely seen him for two days since he's been working on his blog."

"No, I mean the other guy."

Her head jerked off of his shoulder. "What are you talking about? What other guy?"

"You know. Mark Logan."

"Susan's Uncle Mark?" She sat up to look him in the face. "When did he get here?"

"This afternoon." Al also sat up. "I thought you knew. You went upstairs before supper and I heard you talking to him."

"That was Ross. I peeked into his room to see if he wanted a sandwich since he didn't go with Susan and Justin for dinner." Her eyes went round as melons. "If Susan's uncle is here, why didn't he go with them?"

"Maybe he met the Hinkle woman and decided against it," Al replied in a sour tone. "Can't blame the man for that."

"I don't like having a guest in the house I haven't met." Millie threw the comforter off and got out of bed. "Get dressed."

"Why?"

She planted her hands—even the one with the brace, which proved it was nearly healed—on her hips. "Surely you don't expect me to barge into a strange man's bedroom alone."

A good point. Grumbling, he climbed out of bed and pulled on the trousers and shirt he'd removed and tossed in the clothes bin. When Millie reached for a lipstick, he grabbed her arm.

"You're just saying hello and telling him about breakfast."

He thought she might argue, but instead she gave a nod and followed him out of the room. The house was quiet except for the droning voice coming from the television in the Bo Peep room. Upstairs, light showed beneath Mayfield's door, but nothing below Mark's.

"He must already be asleep," Millie whispered. "Maybe we should slip a note under the door telling him breakfast is at nine."

Al pressed an ear to the solid wood. The door, which apparently had not been latched, cracked open.

"Albert!" hissed Millie, grabbing his arm to tug him away.

But something about the stillness from inside that room didn't feel right. Placing a hand on the wood, he pushed it open a couple of inches. "Mark? Are you in there?"

Complete silence. Al opened the door wider, and Millie came to his side as he flipped on the wall switch.

The room was empty.

❈

Millie held the cell phone to her ear and waited for Susan to answer. "Hello?"

Oh good. She sounded wide awake.

"Susan, this is Millie. We were calling about your uncle." She glanced up at Albert, who stood close enough that he could hear both ends of the conversation. She tilted the phone out slightly.

"Uncle Mark?" The young woman's voice sounded surprised.

"We wanted to make sure he's okay. We're going to bed and wondered if we should leave the door unlocked."

"Millie, what are you talking about? Uncle Mark isn't coming until next Friday."

"That's what we thought, but he arrived today. Al met him and showed him to his room, but we haven't seen him since."

After a moment's silence, Susan said slowly, "Daddy said he was coming to Kentucky early so he could go to the races at Churchill Downs. Maybe he was on his way there and decided to stop in Goose Creek to make sure he knew where to come on Friday."

A plausible explanation.

Albert didn't appear convinced. "Why wouldn't he have said something when I showed him his room? When he left he said he was going to look around town. Did he come to see you?"

"No, but I was really busy all day. Maybe he stopped by and I was in the back with a patient. Still, you'd think Alice would have told me I had a visitor."

"Maybe she forgot?" Millie said.

"Maybe." A moment of silence. "Daddy has some dinner thing with clients from the bank tonight, and I hate to bother him. But I'll give him a call in the morning and see if he's heard from Uncle Mark."

"That sounds good." Millie took possession of the phone, and Al stepped away. "I'm sure there's a reasonable explanation."

"Yeah, I'm sure you're right. But Millie? I'd lock the doors tonight."

A prickle marched across the back of Millie's neck. Definitely a good idea.

# Chapter Eighteen

"Fried oatmeal," Millie announced, setting one plate in front of Lorna and one in front of Ross.

Ross looked more relaxed this morning than he had since his arrival. He inspected the dish with apparent interest. "I've never heard of frying oatmeal."

Lorna's eyebrows assumed the shape of the McDonald's arches. "It must be a southern thing. They fry everything down here."

Millie would have disagreed, but Albert was waiting to take her to town for a much-anticipated pedicure appointment, and she didn't have time for a lengthy conversation with Lorna.

"Some people like it with syrup, but I've fixed a dish of cinnamon apples that I think goes nicely on the top." She scooted the bowl within easy reach. "I hope you enjoy it. We're leaving for town."

Lorna twisted in her seat to fix a disbelieving stare on Millie. "Am I to understand you expect us to clear the table? At the price we're paying?"

"Of course not," Millie assured her. "I'll only be gone an hour or so, and I'll take care of the dishes when I get back. The only thing I ask is that you cover the apple dish if there are any left."

With a cheery smile, Millie made a quick exit. She snatched her purse off the kitchen counter and nudged Rufus with the toe of her flip-flop.

"Come on, lazybones. You're going outside to enjoy the sunshine. Maybe you'll find a squirrel or two to chase."

At the word *squirrel*, Rufus's ears perked upright. He rose from his cushion and trotted through the door she held open. Sure enough, he spied a specimen of his arch nemesis in the grass and leaped off the veranda with a ferocious bark.

Albert started the engine when she slid into the car. "How long does a pedicure take?"

"Thirty or forty minutes, maybe. But take your time. Violet's scheduled for one after me, so I plan to stay and chat."

The addition of Tuesday's Day Spa provided the perfect place for the ladies to gather while the men enjoyed their Saturday morning tradition of coffee at the drugstore soda fountain. Millie and Violet had scheduled these pedicures purposefully today in hopes of beginning a new custom. If it caught on, Tuesday would benefit from the additional business.

Albert parked in one of the spaces in front of the Day Spa.

"Would you come inside for a minute?" she asked. "I want you to smell the lavender candle I'm considering buying to burn in the parlor."

He balked. "Fill the house with whatever smelly stuff you want. I don't care."

"But I want to make sure you like it. Some people aren't fond of lavender."

Shrugging, he followed her through the purple door. Inside they found Lulu seated in the pedicure chair. Tuesday perched on a stool at her feet, hunched over her toes.

"Hey, girlie. Haven't seen much of you lately."

Millie crossed the room to give Lulu a careful hug without jostling her foot. "I've been so busy with my guests, I've hardly had time to do anything." She inspected Tuesday's handiwork. "That's a pretty pink."

The massage therapist flashed a smile at her. "It's one of my favorites."

"She's gonna do me a flower too."

Since Tuesday was only on the first foot, that meant she'd be a while longer. Violet would probably be here before Lulu left, the first encounter between the two since the Main Street Program application was filed.

Millie bit down on her lip. Should she say something to try to smooth the way? Lulu *did* ask for help in developing her personal communication skills.

"Um, Violet will be here soon. Would you do me a favor?"

Lulu cocked her head. "Name it, girlie."

"Don't call her Plum." Tuesday interrupted her work to look up, and a question appeared on Lulu's face. "The nickname really annoys her," Millie explained, "and I don't want to see you two at odds over something so silly."

"I understand how she feels." Tuesday plunged the brush into the bright pink bottle of polish. "In high school there was a girl who called me Wednesday." A shudder shook her. "I know she was only teasing, but it made me so mad."

"Thanks for letting me know." Instead of being offended, Lulu's gratitude sounded genuine. "And I'll tell my Honey Bun too."

Al spoke from where he stood in front of the soy candle display. "While you're at it, tell him not to call me Bert."

The door opened and a pair of ladies entered. Millie didn't recognize either of them.

Tuesday turned and called a greeting. "Hello there. Can I help you with something?"

"We're just browsing," one of the women replied.

"Well, browse away. Holler if you have a question." She pointed with the polish brush. "Help yourself to tea or coffee. It's free."

The two exchanged grins, and the one with the darker hair said, "It's exactly the way he described it. So friendly."

The two drifted toward the tea table, and Al approached holding a candle. "Is this the one you want me to smell?"

Millie inspected the sticker on the bottom and nodded. "That's lavender. What do you think?"

He sniffed and then wrinkled his nose. "It reminds me of a doctor's office."

"Now aren't you glad I asked?" She took his arm and guided him back to the candles. "Let's find one you like."

One of the browsers approached. "I love soy candles. Are they homemade?"

"Yes." Millie pointed out Tuesday. "She owns the Day Spa, and she makes the candles and the natural cleansers."

Al made a show of sniffing three candles and then shoved one at her, his impatience apparent. "This one. Come get me when you're ready to go."

Millie took the vanilla candle, a twin to the one she had at home, and returned it to the table.

The dark-haired lady picked it up and smelled it. "Lovely. Beth, try this one."

As Albert left, Violet entered. She smiled at Millie, but when she caught sight of Lulu, the smile dimmed.

"Hello, Violet," called Lulu. "That's a mighty pretty shirt you've got on. And your hair looks extra nice today, like you just left the hairdresser."

Millie winced. They needed to have a talk about overdoing the compliments. But at least Violet's thank-you was polite enough to be considered cordial.

Beth approached the table and picked up a candle to sniff. "Do y'all live here?"

"Yes, we do."

The friend's smile widened. "It's such a charming town, so quaint and cute."

"We like it." On her way to get a cup of tea, Violet asked, "Where are you from?"

"Cincinnati," Beth answered. "We didn't even know this town was here until yesterday, so Lisa and I thought we'd drive down and see if it's as sweet as it sounded."

Lisa selected a bright red pillar. "Can you tell us where the Goose Creek B&B is?"

Millie nearly dropped her purse. "Excuse me?"

"The Goose Creek B&B," she repeated. "We wanted to go by and see if Mrs. Richardson would give us a tour of the house."

Lulu piped up from the corner. "Why don't you ask her right now? You're talking to her."

Both ladies eyed Millie with obvious delight. "You're Mrs. Richardson?"

"I am." The conversation was approaching the surreal. Who were these people? "I'd be happy to show you the house, but I can't imagine where you heard about it. The B&B isn't scheduled to open for another two years."

Now they looked confused. "But don't you have people staying there now?" Beth asked.

She could explain, but she wasn't sure she should. Coming on the heels of Susan's mysterious Uncle Mark, she was inclined to be a little suspicious. "How do you know that?"

"From an article on the Internet," Beth said.

Millie must have looked confused because Lisa offered an explanation.

"Now that the weather's finally nice, we were looking for someplace to take a day trip, maybe do some shopping and have lunch. So last night we Googled small towns in Kentucky and Ohio, and found a blog that has several articles about Goose Creek."

"The author said he was staying at the Goose Creek B&B," Beth added.

Relieved, Millie relaxed. Ross had been working hard on his blogs, but she'd no idea he'd already written several.

"What fun," Tuesday exclaimed. "We're famous on the Internet."

"He described the town perfectly," Lisa said. "And he mentioned this Day Spa, and the drugstore, and the quirky shop across the street."

"We're heading there next." Beth gave a little laugh. "Imagine a store called the Freckled Frog."

"It's a fun place," Lulu said. "Packed to the rafters with stuff you won't see anywhere else."

The image of Chester rose in Millie's mind. That was certainly true.

"Do you think it would be possible to take a tour of your B&B?" Lisa held the cinnamon candle in both hands up to her nose, peering at Millie over the top. "We don't want to be a bother, of course."

She opened her mouth to tell them she'd be happy to show them around, but never got the opportunity. The door flew open, and Albert burst through.

"It's Uncle Mark. He's across the street."

She rushed to the front window, joined by Violet and the two curious visitors from Cincinnati.

"Who's Uncle Mark?" Violet asked.

"Susan's uncle." Millie unzipped her purse and rummaged inside for her cell phone. "He showed up at the B&B yesterday and checked in but then disappeared. We thought he'd gone to the races in Louisville." She dialed Susan's cell phone number, and when the young woman answered, spoke in a rush. "Can you get away? Your uncle is on Main Street next to the Frog."

"I'm on my way," Susan said.

"We're at Tuesday's." Millie dropped the phone back in her purse.

Her pedicure apparently finished, Lulu joined them at the window, doing an awkward duckwalk in disposable foam shoes. Tuesday slid in beside Violet to form a line of seven spectators, all watching as the man across the street bent for a close examination of the corner of the crumbling building next to Frieda's.

Violet lifted a finger and stabbed at the glass. "Hey, that's the guy we saw yesterday."

Millie had just come to the same realization. "And he's still taking pictures."

The stranger pulled out his cell phone and snapped a shot of the corner.

"The guy's a weirdo. I want to know what he's up to." Al reached for the door, but Millie snatched his arm back.

"We should wait for Susan. We don't want to offend her uncle a week before her wedding."

Beth turned to Lisa with a giggle. "How exciting! I'm so glad we drove down."

*Exciting* was not the term Millie would have chosen.

They didn't have long to wait. Susan had apparently drawn on her skills as a high school track sprinter, for she rounded the corner a moment later.

Al opened the door. "In here," he said in a stage whisper.

Susan entered, her gaze circling the room. "Where's Uncle Mark?"

"Over there." Millie pointed at the man, who now stood in front of the Freckled Frog, making a study of the doorposts.

Susan studied the man. "That's not Uncle Mark." She shook her head. "I've never seen that man before in my life."

Spider legs crept up Millie's spine. "Then why was he at my house yesterday pretending to be your uncle?"

"Enough." Albert stiffened his spine, his expression as stern as Millie had ever seen it. "I'm going to confront him."

He stomped out the door, and Millie called after him, "Albert, be careful."

"He ought not approach a stranger alone," Lulu said. "I wish my Honey Bun was here."

"You're right," Violet agreed. "The man might be a lunatic or something."

Millie opened the door and ran after her husband, Violet close on her heels.

"There's safety in numbers, girlies," came Lulu's voice.

Millie glanced back and found herself at the head of a parade of women, Lulu bringing up the rear with her odd, mincing step and her toes arched high.

"Not a lot of support in these things," she said as she stepped carefully over the railroad tracks.

"Somebody better record this," Beth suggested. "If a fight breaks out, we'll want to be able to prove to the police whose fault it was."

"We can do it on our cell phones." An excited giggle sounded from Lisa's direction. "Who knows? It might go viral on YouTube."

"You there." Albert called to the man from several yards away. "What are you doing?"

The fake Uncle Mark swiveled, eyes going wide when he found himself confronted by seven people. "Just taking a few pictures of the buildings."

Susan marched up to stand beside Albert. "You're not my Uncle Mark."

A shamefaced expression crept over his face. "My name's Mark Logan, but I'm nobody's uncle."

"You deliberately misrepresented yourself yesterday at my home." Albert drew himself up. "Perhaps we need to call the police to get to the bottom of this."

Cell phones held aloft, Lisa and Beth stepped to one side so they could get a clear shot of the confrontation.

"I did no such thing." He lowered his head a touch but still looked Albert in the eye. "You made an assumption, and it's true I didn't correct you. To be honest, I was reeling from shock."

The door to the Freckled Frog opened, and Frieda stuck her head out. "Is there a problem out here?"

Mark Logan whirled on her. "There certainly is. Mr. and Mrs. Richardson have destroyed the integrity of an historic building."

Millie gasped and then marched up to stand beside Albert. "What are you talking about?"

"Mrs. Richardson?" When she nodded, he straightened. "I'm

from the Heritage Council. I'm following up on your application to become a part of the Main Street Program."

Words failed her. Lulu duckwalked forward to stand beside her.

"You're an inspector?" Violet asked.

"I'm a freelance preservationist." Head held high enough to give haughty Lorna a run for her money, he fixed a contemptuous glare on Millie. "The Council enlisted my assistance since you requested that your application be expedited, and they're shorthanded. When I arrived at that lovely Victorian-era home yesterday and saw the way you've defiled it, I was appalled."

The Cincinnati tourists, their delight apparent, swung their cell phones toward her.

Millie drew herself upright. "I don't know what you're talking about. The house was in terrible shape when we bought it. We're restoring it a bit at a time."

"No, madam, you are not *restoring* it. You're desecrating it." He speared her with a sharp gaze. "You put *asphalt* shingles on the roof."

Millie risked a glance at Albert. The use of less expensive roofing material had been at his insistence.

With jerky motions, Mark Logan held his notepad aloft and flipped several pages. "The home was built in 1892. Asphalt shingles did not come into use until the early 1900s." He rounded on Albert. "And you, sir, want to continue ravaging the house by tearing up vintage poplar flooring to install *laminate*."

"Albert!" Millie turned a stern look his way. "I thought we'd agreed to nix that idea."

He shoved a hand in his pocket and started to speak, but Mark cut him off.

"After witnessing the horrors being done to that beautiful home, I knew I'd better take a closer look at the downtown historic district." He waved his pen around, encompassing the buildings up and down Main Street. "Precious historic resources here are in serious decline. Just look at that." He pointed toward the sagging awning over the used bookstore and then at the crumbling facade of the vacant building next to the Frog. "Disgraceful."

"It costs money to do all those repairs," Tuesday said. "I had to take out a loan to fix up the Day Spa."

Mark rounded on her, eyes bulging. "You're responsible for that… that…sacrilege?"

"Hey," Susan said. "My fiancé did the work on that building, and he did a great job."

"While I will admit the restoration work is acceptable, the color is entirely unacceptable."

Tuesday's lower lip protruded as she glanced toward her building. "You don't like what I've done with it?"

"Madam, it's *purple*. Structures built in the 1800s were not purple."

Frieda folded her arms and gave a prim smile. "If you'll remember, I advised against purple from the outset."

"And take this building, for instance." Mark waved at the Freckled Frog. "The trim is all wrong for that era. And where did you get that door? From the Penney's catalog?"

Frieda went statue-still.

"Now hold up there a minute, cowboy." Shuffling on the lilac-colored pedicure slippers, Lulu planted herself in front of the man. "That's what the Main Street Program is all about. It's us committing to do the fixing-up, and you to do the helping."

He eyed her. "The Main Street Program's goal is economic development through historic preservation. What we have here isn't preservation."

"Well, now, that's where we disagree." Lulu cocked her head on her long neck. "I seem to remember a couple of different definitions in the research I did." She held up a hand and raised a finger with each point. "We can *conserve* a building, which means we won't let it get any worse than it already is. We can *restore* it back to the way it looked when it was first built. We can *preserve* it, which means do repairs but update it to today's standards. Or we can *rehabilitate* it, which means it's gonna be used for something different than it was intended to be."

Caution stole over the man's expression, and Frieda looked openly impressed.

Lulu continued. "What we've done here in Goose Creek is preserving, and that's okay." She held up a hand. "I'm not saying we don't have more work to do. That's where the Main Street Program's gonna help. But there's not a rule anywhere saying we have to match paint colors and such."

A crooked vein appeared in Mark's temple, and his face darkened. "I've been asked by the Heritage Council for my opinion, and that's what I will report. I'm a historical preservationist who happens to believe that the purist approach is best."

Lulu planted a lanky arm on her hip. "Well excuse me for saying so, mister, but I think you're a *hysterical* preservationist who happens to be wrong. And I'm darn well gonna share that opinion with the director of the Heritage Council."

While the man sputtered, Frieda and Tuesday applauded. The delighted Cincinnati tourists, their phones pointed at Lulu, grinned ear to ear. Millie slipped an arm around Lulu's waist and squeezed. Sometimes one must throw diplomacy to the wind, as her friend had just done.

Apparently at a loss for words, Mark Logan turned on his heel and marched away. The little group on the sidewalk watched him get into a car and leave.

Beth punched a button on her cell phone and beamed at her friend. "I got every bit of that. I wonder if Mr. Mayfield would want to use it on his blog."

"I'm posting mine on Facebook," Lisa said.

The two pocketed their phones and, with a wave, entered the Freckled Frog.

Violet turned to Lulu and stuck out a hand. "I was wrong. You're the best Main Street Manager Goose Creek could have."

"You sure are." Tuesday smiled widely.

"I concur." Frieda glanced in the direction Mark Logan had gone. "If our application is approved, that is."

"Oh, it will be approved." Millie gave Lulu's waist another squeeze. "The director of the Heritage Council is a reasonable man. We'll talk to him." She turned a scowl on Albert. "We are *not* installing laminate in our house."

"Okay, okay." Holding up both hands in a gesture of submission, he backed away. "I'm going to Cardwell's for coffee now. And I'm not getting decaf," he added with a touch of defiance.

Millie didn't argue. After that encounter, she could use a shot of caffeine herself.

# Chapter Nineteen

The moment Susan opened her eyes, an electric thrill shot from her head to her toes.

*It's my wedding day!*

She sat up on the foldout sofa that had been her bed for the past two years and glanced around the empty apartment. The last of her things had been packed off to her new home last night after a quiet dinner with Justin, Daddy, and Uncle Mark—the *real* Uncle Mark. Ross had opted for a sandwich in his room while he worked on another blog post about Goose Creek. Susan had been surprised when Aunt Lorna declined to join them, claiming that she needed a good night's rest before the *big event*. Susan raised her arms and stretched. The euphemism might not be true in terms of size, but was certainly appropriate in terms of impact. At eleven-thirty this morning she would become Mrs. Justin Hinkle. Truly the biggest and best event of her life.

Her phone rang. Probably Justin, calling to wish her a happy wedding day. She grabbed the charger cable, pulled the phone toward her, and glanced at the screen.

Not Justin. Millie.

"Hello?"

"You'd better get over here," Millie said with no preamble, her tone tight with tension.

Alarm pinged in Susan's brain. "Is something wrong?"

"She's done something you're not going to like."

The *she* could only mean one person. Aunt Lorna.

She leaped out of bed. "I'm on my way."

❄

Millie stood in the center of the backyard while a pair of delivery men marched past her carrying an eight-foot wedding arch.

"Right over there," Lorna directed, pointing toward the gazebo. "Set it right up against the opening."

They did as directed, and she stepped back to inspect it, a finger across her lips. "Millie, what do you think?"

"I think Susan is going to throw a fit."

"Leave Susan to me. Does it look centered to you?"

Aware that she tread a dangerous path, Millie considered not answering.

She and Albert had been awakened at six thirty by the loud *thump-thump* of a carton being dragged down the stairs. They'd thrown on their robes and exited their bedroom to find Lorna dragging a box through the kitchen door onto the veranda.

Millie glanced in that direction, where no less than eight good-sized boxes had been piled. Would Susan think her complicit in the blatant hijacking of her wedding?

Albert appeared at her side and pressed a coffee mug into her hands. "Want me to toast you a bagel for breakfast?"

"No thanks." She took the coffee, grateful for something to help clear her mind, but a mass of knots had lodged in her stomach, and she didn't think she could eat a bite.

"A little to the left," Lorna directed, and the men obeyed. "Perfect. Now, the flower stands will go on each side."

"What in the world is happening here?"

Millie and Albert turned to find Susan approaching from around the delivery truck, her jaw dangling.

Millie rushed to her side. "I had nothing to do with it. I promise."

Susan passed her as though in a daze, her gaze fixed on the arch and the two white pillars nearby.

"There you are, Susan dear." Lorna gathered the stunned young woman into a hug. "Nature has certainly smiled on your big day. The Weather Channel says sunshine all day, hardly any wind, and low seventies. Perfect for an outdoor wedding."

"I can't believe it. Justin said I'd slide down a slippery slope, but I didn't. I conceded a few things, true, but I held firm. Not a wedding. Nothing elaborate. Just a simple ceremony." She turned a bewildered gaze on Lorna. "You did it anyway."

"Now, my dear." Lorna took her hand and held it between both of hers. "It's only a few decorations. Just wait until you see the tulle draped across the arch and the flowers sprayed ar—"

"Flowers?" Susan took a backward step. "You ordered flowers?"

"Not real flowers. Silk ones. A wide variety, so you can choose the colors. We'll return the ones we don't use."

Now Millie understood the multitude of boxes in the Bo Peep room. "You said all those deliveries were wedding gifts."

"They are." Lorna patted the hand she still held. "I'm gifting them with a wedding. Oh, and I've got several things to decorate the table as well. Darling little crystal vases and a lace runner."

Susan whirled on Millie with an accusation. "You said we were having finger food."

"We are! Little sandwiches and fruit and a relish tray. And I made the wedding cake myself." Dismayed, Millie looked toward the archway. Her homemade cake would appear pitiful flanked by crystal vases.

She looked around for Albert and found him seated on the veranda, his feet propped up on the railing, sipping coffee and watching them with a wide smile, giving every indication of enjoying the spectacle.

The rumble of a motorcycle reached them, and moments later

Justin's Harley roared into view. He cut the engine and kicked down the stand, standing to take his helmet off.

"No, no, no!" Lorna dashed across the yard, flapping her hands like she was shooing chickens. "You can't see the bride before the wedding. It's bad luck."

"First off, I don't believe in luck." Justin grinned at Susan. "I believe in love. And second, we don't have to worry about that since we're not having a wedding." He looked at the arch. "Or are we?"

Susan gave a helpless shrug. "I didn't think so."

The fingers clutching his helmet turned white. When he spoke to his aunt, it was with an obvious attempt to maintain an even tone. "We've told you over and over what we want for our wedding, but you've fought us at every turn."

"My boy, I'm only trying to help. Your dear mother allowed me the privilege of helping to plan her wedding, and it was lovely." She turned to Susan. "Since your poor mother can't be here, I wanted to do the same for you."

Millie caught the gleam of moisture in Susan's eye, and her heart twisted. How painful it must be for a girl to miss her mother on her wedding day.

Justin seemed unaffected. He answered in the same stern tone. "It's not that we don't appreciate your kindness, but we spent a long time talking about this. We both own busy businesses, and we didn't want to deal with all the stress and expense of a big wedding."

"But you've had neither." Lorna threw her hands wide. "I've done it all."

Turning his back on her, Justin grabbed both of Susan's hands and held them. "Let's go with our original plan. I'll call Reverend Hollister and tell him we'll be at his office at eleven thirty."

For a long moment, no one spoke. Millie found herself unable to watch as the two young people exchanged a deep gaze, silently communicating in the way only couples can. Lorna sucked in a noisy breath and held it.

Finally Susan cast a glance toward the arch in front of the gazebo. Was there a hint of longing in her eyes?

"Since everything's already done," she said slowly, "there really isn't anything to stress about."

Lorna released her breath with a delighted exclamation. A knot unwound in Millie's stomach.

Susan turned to Lorna with a fierce gaze. "But promise me one thing. You haven't invited any other guests, have you?"

Lorna placed a hand over her heart. "You have my word." She hesitated. "Unless you count the photographer, who will be here at ten."

"All right." Justin pulled his bride-to-be into an embrace. "I guess we're having a wedding."

# Chapter Twenty

Millie clipped the stem off of the last creamy silk rose, positioned it in the icing of her cake next to the rest, and stepped back to admire her handiwork. Perfect. She indulged in a moment of self-congratulations as she examined the table. Lorna's satin tablecloth and lace runner certainly added a touch of elegance to the already beautiful room. The crystal vases were stunning, and a near-perfect match to the sparkling chandelier. She half-wished she could keep them, but the telltale sticker on the box identified them as part of Waterford's Lismore collection. They must have cost a fortune.

With a final glance, she headed for the bedroom to check on Albert. She found him in the bathroom, struggling with his tie.

"I don't see why I have to wear a suit. It's a backyard wedding, for goodness sake."

She pushed his hands out of the way and tied it properly. "We're the host and hostess. We can't serve our guests in jeans and T-shirts."

"When I agreed to buy this house, I never expected to become a server."

"Stop grumbling." Stepping back, she smiled at him. "There. You look like the lord of the manor house."

A frantic barking from the direction of the kitchen interrupted whatever Albert might have answered.

"What's got Rufus so upset?" she asked.

"He probably saw a squirrel through the storm door. We'd better go calm him before he goes through the screen after it."

Millie followed Al into the kitchen, and they both stopped short when they caught sight of Junior Watson standing on the veranda, peering inside through the back door.

Millie did a double take. Junior had slicked his hair down with a shiny gel and wore a clean button-up shirt beneath his overalls.

Millie hooked Rufus by the collar and dragged him back.

Justin, who had been upstairs dressing for his wedding, appeared behind them. "Junior? What are you doing here?"

"We'uns is here for the weddin', only I ain't sure what to do with my goat."

The words fell on Millie's ears but failed to make sense. "Your goat?"

"Yes'm," he said through the screen. "It's kinda skittish around all them dogs."

"All them—" Millie, Albert, and Justin rushed to the door and crowded each other to look through the screen.

The backyard had undergone a transformation. Not the one that had occurred this morning, with the appearance of the wedding arch and a profusion of billowy tulle, flowers, and white satin bows.

People and animals filled the green grassy area in a crowded jumble. Millie caught sight of Larry Greely and his bird dog, Bella, standing beside Edith Bowling and her Newfie, Boomer. Beneath one large oak, Delores Barnes held her fluffy Arnold, and next to her Mrs. Pennyweather stood with her Siamese. A brown blur raced across the lawn, and Millie identified Benji the Yorkie in hot pursuit of poor Pepe the Chihuahua. Their owners ran after them, the heels of Nina's sandals ripping through the white aisle runner that the bride would soon walk down. The photographer, carrying a giant camera, stood to one side, capturing the chaos on film.

"The paper said to bring a pet." Junior ducked his head. "I don't really have no pet, so I figgered my goat would do in a pinch." He looked up at Justin. "I wouldn't miss your wedding to Dr. Susan for anything."

Justin turned to Millie. "You'd better go warn Susan. I'll get to the bottom of this."

Millie hurried away.

❄

Al opened the screen door and followed Justin outside.

"No," he told Rufus, when the creature would have wiggled between his legs. "Stay."

He received a defiant doggie stare, but at least the animal halted and allowed him to shut the door.

Sure enough, tied with a rope to one of the veranda posts stood a nervous-looking goat, its hooves tapping against the decorative pavers as it kept a cautious eye on Edith's ginormous bearlike dog.

Justin raked fingers through his hair. "You mentioned a paper?"

"Yep. Found it in my mailbox a few days back. Here 'tis."

Junior pulled a crumpled sheet of paper from his pocket and handed it over. Al read over Justin's shoulder.

> *Justin Hinkle and Susan Jeffries*
> *request the honor*
> *of your presence as they celebrate*
> *their marriage on*
> *Saturday, May 27, at 11:30 in the morning.*
> *The wedding will be at*
> *1427 Ash Street,*
> *Goose Creek, Kentucky.*
> *Don't RSVP, but bring your pets.*

The invitation had been printed on letterhead from the Goose Creek Animal Clinic.

Justin shook his head. "I don't understand. It's obviously a fake, but feel that." He handed the paper to Al, who ran a finger across the raised lettering at the top of the page.

"Feels like real letterhead," Al said.

They were interrupted by a shout. "Tootsie Wootsie, you come back here!"

A gray cat dashed across the yard, and Tuesday Love rounded the corner of the house at a run, barefoot and carrying a pair of high-heeled sandals.

Behind Al, a canine bellow alerted him to impending disaster. He leaped toward the door, but before he took more than a step, Rufus soared through the screen. He landed with a crash that drew the attention of everyone in the yard, righted himself, and darted after the cat. The feline leaped for a tree and soared upward just as Rufus reached the trunk.

An uproar of shouts, screeches, hisses, and barks ensued, along with the bleating from the terrified goat.

Beneath it all, a completely different noise reached Al's ears. The high-pitched sound of juvenile laughter.

Catching Justin's eye, Al gestured for him to follow. Together they crept in the opposite direction, around the corner by the driveway and past the front porch. At the far edge, Al motioned for Justin to stop. Together they craned their necks and peered around the corner.

Just as Al expected.

Overcome with giggles, the culprits, hidden behind a row of giant lilac bushes, were so involved in watching the chaos they were completely unaware of Al's and Justin's approach until it was too late.

Justin grabbed each of them by the collars of their T-shirts. "Got you."

At least Al had the satisfaction of seeing their laughter replaced by identical expressions of sheer panic.

❧

"Hooligans!" Lorna's voice echoed in the confines of the parlor. She shook an accusing finger in the boys' faces. "You deserve to be locked away like the delinquents you are."

Millie almost felt sorry for the Wainright boys. They, more than most, understood the threat of a juvenile detention center. They sat huddled together in the center of the sofa, wretched and despondent.

"What were you thinking?" Susan paced back and forth in front of the fireplace, her creamy white skirt billowing with every step. "Why do you hate me so much?"

Shoulders hunched, Forest shook his head. "We don't hate you, Dr. Susan."

"We like you," Heath said.

"Then why would you purposefully try to sabotage my wedding?"

Heath whispered to his brother. "What's that mean?"

"She thinks we wanted to wreck things," Forest answered.

"No ma'am." Heath raised earnest eyes. "We heard you talking about how you didn't have any friends to invite on account of most of your friends being animals."

Forest nodded. "We got to thinking that animals are people too, so why can't they have a little fun every now and then?"

Justin, who had taken up a stance in the corner after delivering the miscreants to the parlor to face their feminine interrogators, spoke up. "You expect us to believe you did this out of the goodness of your hearts so dogs and cats could attend a party?"

The two exchanged guilty glances.

"Nah," Forest admitted. "Mostly we thought it would be funny."

Millie turned away to hide her smile. They had certainly achieved their goal, though it might be a while before either Susan or Justin were able to see the humor of the situation.

"Funny?" Lorna drew herself up and glowered down at the pair. "You *stole* letterhead from a business and sent a fake communication. You could be prosecuted for forgery, mail fraud, and theft."

Forest's head jerked upright. "I didn't steal nothing. She gave it to me."

He pointed at Susan, who nodded. "He's right. But I thought you were going to draw horses, not print a fake wedding invitation." She lifted the crumpled paper she held. "How'd you do this anyway? With the exception of some wording problems, it looks authentic."

"We looked up wedding invitations on the Internet and added the stuff about the pets."

"We've got a printer at home." Heath shrugged. "Paper's paper."

The parlor door opened, and Al led a furious Alice into the room. Catching sight of their mother, the young criminals sank even lower.

Alice marched over and planted herself directly in front of them. "You two are grounded for the rest of your lives. No TV, no tablets, no Game Boys, nothing. You'll be lucky if you're allowed out of your bedroom before you graduate from high school." She turned to Susan and, covering her mouth with one hand, extended the other. "I can't tell you how sorry I am. I don't know how I can ever make up for this, but I'll find a way." Tears choked her voice. "And I'll resign. As soon as you can find a replacement, you'll never have to see any of us again."

Millie's heart went out to the wretched woman. Obviously mortified at her boys' behavior, she must feel like such a failure.

"Oh, Alice, you'll do no such thing." Susan stepped forward and gathered the weeping woman in an embrace. "How could I ever manage without you and Millie? Losing you over this prank really would be a disaster."

Breaking into the emotional embrace, Justin put a hand on his soon-to-be wife's shoulder. "Can we delay this conversation a bit? We've got a herd of animals and people in the backyard waiting for a wedding that they think they were invited to, and a minister who informed me he has an appointment with his barber this afternoon that he doesn't want to reschedule. And besides…" The tender look he fixed on Susan would melt any woman's heart. "I don't want to wait a minute longer to marry you."

Millie thought of the lovely table laid out with crystal and silver. "And what about after the ceremony? We don't have enough food to feed all those people."

"I have an idea." Susan's grin as she gazed at Justin revealed not a smidge of stress, only love. "Let's invite everyone to join us at the Whistlestop for lunch. We can take the cake and cut it there."

"Perfect." He held out a crooked elbow. "Shall we go get married, Dr.-Almost-Mrs. Hinkle?"

Susan looped her arm through his, and they headed for the door.

"Wait!" Lorna halted them with an impervious shout, eyeing the guilty pair on the sofa. "I demand to know what's to be done with *them*."

Albert, who had remained silent through the entire encounter, piped up with a suggestion. "Let them work to make up for their mischief. I have the perfect job to start them off." A devilish grin spread across his face as he whipped something from behind his back. Millie recognized the item instantly—a box of doggie cleanup bags. He leveled a stern gaze on the boys. "There's going to be a huge mess in my backyard. Before you leave, I expect it to look like no animal was ever here."

# Chapter Twenty-One

The day Al had looked forward to for three weeks finally arrived. The guests were checking out, and he and Millie were about to get their house back.

They stood side by side on the porch to bid farewell to Thomas Jeffries and his friend, Mark Fenrod.

"You have a beautiful home, Mrs. Richardson, and you're a marvelous cook." Mark rubbed a hand over his protruding middle. "It's not often a man is treated to eggs Benedict, and that was the best I've ever tasted."

Millie awarded him a gracious smile. True, she'd had to get up much earlier than she wanted in order to prepare the special last-morning breakfast, but as Lorna had told her, "All the best B&Bs serve eggs Benedict."

"Thank you. I hope you'll come and stay with us again when we're officially open."

"I look forward to it." Shaking Albert's hand, he headed for his car.

Instead of shaking her hand, Thomas pulled her into a quick hug. "I can't thank you enough for all you've done for Susan. She thinks so highly of you, almost as if you were family."

"We feel the same for her," Millie assured him.

"And thank you for hosting the wedding. In spite of everything, I think it turned out well." He cocked his head. "Weird, but well."

Millie laughed. "As long as Susan and Justin are happy, we are too."

Thomas pulled a checkbook out of his pocket and asked Albert, "What do I owe you? I want to pick up the tab for Mark too."

They had discussed the matter last night in bed. Al shook his head. "Nothing. As Millie said, we consider Susan and Justin part of the family. That makes you a de facto relative."

From the look on his face, Thomas was prepared to argue the point.

Millie forestalled the disagreement. "If you force a check on us, we'll only tear it up after you've gone." She grinned. "If you want to repay us, tell your friends about our B&B after we open."

"It's a deal." He shook Albert's hand and trotted down the stairs. Sliding behind the wheel of his Lexus, he followed his friend down the driveway.

They started to enter the house when the door opened and Ross appeared, lugging his knapsack and laptop case. The difference in his appearance this morning compared to the day of his arrival was remarkable. A true smile rested easily on his face, and he held himself upright instead of slouching. Of course, the haircut Lorna had paid for a few days before the wedding helped, but the change went deeper than appearances.

Millie took his hand and held it. "It has been a pleasure getting to know you, Ross. And I've been meaning to tell you that I'm following your blog. You're a good writer."

A blush stained his cheeks. "Thank you, Mrs. Richardson."

"She's not the only one," Albert added. "I was talking to a couple of the guys at the Whistlestop last night, and they tell me business has picked up in the past week. Tourists coming to the Creek, spending money and exclaiming how the place is just like they read on the Internet. Seems you've got quite a following."

"I wasn't going to say anything, but…" He lowered his gaze. "I received an email a few days ago asking me to submit my résumé and samples. I did, and Friday I got a writing assignment from National Geographic's *Traveler* magazine. They're sending me to Europe."

Millie clapped her hands over her mouth and squealed. "That's wonderful, Ross! Congratulations. But why didn't you tell us then?"

He shrugged. "I didn't want to steal Justin and Susan's thunder. It was their big day, not mine."

Al shook his hand. "I plan on doing some traveling myself when I retire. Looking forward to reading your articles. When the B&B opens, maybe you'll write another piece about us."

"Consider it done." His gaze rose and swept the height of the house. "It'll be a pleasure to recommend this place and its excellent hosts."

He descended the stairs and, tossing his bags into the backseat of his beat-up vehicle, gave a final wave. At the end of the driveway, he swerved onto the grass to make way for a limousine, the black paint shining in the late morning sun.

On cue, the door opened, and Miss Hinkle exited the house. She swept across the porch to gather Millie in a smothering hug.

"Millie dear, it has been an absolute pleasure. Things were a touch rough at first, but you've the good sense to listen to sound advice. This morning's breakfast was…" She kissed her fingertips. "Well done, my dear. Well done."

With her departure imminent, Al was able to generate an almost pleasant attitude. "Can I help bring down your luggage?"

"No need. Mr. Jeffries and Mr. Fenrod carried the bulk of it down and—" She waved an imperious hand at the limo driver, who had just parked his car. "Young man, my luggage is just inside," she called.

The formally dressed driver nodded and entered the house.

Miss Hinkle turned to Millie. "FedEx will arrive tomorrow to pick up the rest of my things. You'll find everything clearly marked and prepaid."

"I'll see to it," Millie promised.

Since she'd brought up the subject of payment, Al didn't hesitate to press the matter. "About your bill. Will you be paying with cash or a check?"

"I have it right here." She snapped open her purse and extracted a sealed envelope. "I think you'll find everything in order."

"And you paid Mayfield's tab as well?" Though Millie tossed a quick glare in his direction, Al wouldn't put it past the woman to pull a fast one in regard to her nephew's bill.

She drew up to her full height. "Every penny is accounted for, I assure you."

The driver made his third and final trip from the house and stowed the last of her luggage in the trunk. Then he opened the passenger door with a flourish and stood at near-attention. Al glimpsed an opulent interior with lush leather seats and a center console.

Miss Hinkle smothered Millie in a final hug. "My dear, you've the makings of a fine B&B hostess. I've enjoyed my stay thoroughly."

"Thank you, Lorna." Millie extricated herself from the woman's grip.

When she turned to him, Al stepped back lest she try to hug him as well. "Have a safe trip."

"Thank you," she answered, her nose high.

Posture erect, she descended the porch stairs, turned for one final look at the house, and then settled herself in the car. The driver closed the door, rounded the front, and took his place behind the wheel. As the limo pulled away, a final weight lifted from Al's shoulders.

"Alone at last." He nodded toward the envelope. "Better open that."

She tore the envelope and extracted a single sheet of paper. Al's suspicions were confirmed when she unfolded it and no check fluttered out.

Eyes moving as she read, her jaw dropped. "I don't believe it."

"What?"

Millie looked up at him. "All those so-called gifts? She charged us for every one. Take a look."

Al snatched the paper and scanned the itemized invoice. "Sixteen hundred dollars for a silver tea set? That's outrageous." He looked up in the direction the limo had gone. "We should chase her down and demand payment."

The love of his life, who was far too softhearted, appeared hesitant. "I don't know."

"Millie!" He stiffened his spine to its full extent. "After all the complaining she did about our rates, she stiffed us for the bill. It's an outrage!"

"I know, but…" White teeth appeared and clamped down on her plump lower lip. "Honestly, we're not officially even a B&B yet. We haven't had any inspections, nor have we even applied for a license. Really, we're lucky no one was injured because I doubt if we have the right kind of insurance."

All that made sense, but Al couldn't let go of the indignity of three solid weeks of humiliation at the Hinkle woman's hand.

An idea occurred to him.

"We'll confiscate her belongings." He smiled, triumphant. "All the stuff she bought that's waiting to be shipped to her? We'll sell it on eBay."

Millie appeared ready to argue, but then her expression cleared. "I'll leave that up to you, Albert. Do whatever you think is right. At the moment I'm in too good a mood to worry about it." She drew in a deep breath and blew it out. "At least I've learned something from this practice run."

"What's that?"

Her grin became sheepish. "Running a B&B is a bit more involved than I expected."

Al felt an I-told-you-so opportunity coming on. "So are you saying I was right? That we should have stuck to our agreed-upon plan of opening *after* retirement?" He gave her a piercing look. "That you won't invite any more guests to stay without checking with me *first*?"

"What I'm saying is…" She placed a hand on his chest and gazed up at him with a look that never failed to melt him. "I'm sorry."

Ah, the magic words. They worked both ways. Al wrapped his arms around her and drew her close.

"We're finally alone." She nestled her cheek against his shoulder. "Doesn't it feel good?"

With a wolfish grin, he pulled back to look her in the eye. "Care to celebrate the empty nest?"

In answer, she placed a fingertip on his chest, hooked his shirt, and pulled him toward her for a kiss.

## Final Bill for Lorna Hinkle

Lorna Hinkle, 22 nights in the
Little Bo Peep room @ $150 per night . . . . . . . . . . . . . . . .$3,300.00

Ross Mayfield, 14 nights in the
Little Boy Blue room @ $150 per night. . . . . . . . . . . . . . . $2,100.00

Total Lodging. . . . . . . . . . . . . . . . . . . . . . . . . . . . . . . . . . . . . . . .**$5,400.00**

Regents mirror . . . . . . . . . . . . . . . . . . . . . . . . . . . . . . . . . . . . $306.99

Egyptian velour jacquard towels (12 sets). . . . . . . . . . . . . . $719.99

Bryn wing chair recliner . . . . . . . . . . . . . . . . . . . . . . . . . . . . .$849.99

5 x 8 area rug. . . . . . . . . . . . . . . . . . . . . . . . . . . . . . . . . . . . . . . $419.99

Sterling silver candelabra . . . . . . . . . . . . . . . . . . . . . . . . . . . .$155.00

Hand-thrown pottery sculpture (one of a kind). . . . . . . . $300.00

Lenox Queen Anne oblong silver serving tray . . . . . . . . . $285.00

Lenox Queen Anne oblong silver chafing dish. . . . . . . . . $325.00

Sterling silver tea set . . . . . . . . . . . . . . . . . . . . . . . . . . . . . . .$1,650.00

Satin tablecloth. . . . . . . . . . . . . . . . . . . . . . . . . . . . . . . . . . . . . $32.99

Handmade lace table runner. . . . . . . . . . . . . . . . . . . . . . . . . . $47.99

Waterford crystal vases (2). . . . . . . . . . . . . . . . . . . . . . . . . . . $250.00

Silk flower arrangements for dining room . . . . . . . . . . . . $147.00

Sales tax and delivery charges. . . . . . . . . . . . . . . . . . . . . . . . $395.14

Total Gifts for the Goose Creek B&B . . . . . . . . . . . . . . . . . **$5,885.08**

Difference. . . . . . . . . . . . . . . . . . . . . . . . . . . . . . . . . . . . . . . . . . **(-$485.08)**

*No need to reimburse me the difference, Millie dear. Consider it a gratuity.*
*Sincerely,*
*LH*

# Acknowledgments

Al and Millie have become such a huge part of my life while writing the books in this series, I miss them when I've typed *The End*. They feel real to me. Their marriage is made up of the best parts of my relationship with my husband, Ted. Honestly, dear reader, if Al Richardson has captured even a smidge of your admiration, you would love my Ted. He's one of the most amazing men I know, and I'm so grateful to him for supporting me and my writing career.

Even though the book you've just read is fiction, I went to a lot of trouble to research the details around which the story centers. I owe a debt of gratitude to Craig Potts, the executive director of the Kentucky Heritage Council, who carved a significant portion of time out of his schedule to describe the purpose of the Heritage Council and told me about the Main Street Program. As you know, the information he provided fueled a large part of the story you've just read.

During my research I visited the most amazing B&B in Frankfort, Kentucky. The Meeting House is run by Gary and Rose Burke, a couple who really could have been models for Al and Millie if I'd met them before I wrote the first book in this series. They spent several hours introducing me to their awesome historic house and telling me their stories. Plus, they fed me some of the best meals to be found in Kentucky. Consider this a recommendation: If you find yourself in the central Kentucky area, you absolutely *must* visit the Meeting House for breakfast or lunch, or stay a night in their B&B.

I'm also deeply grateful to my friends Anna Zogg and Marilynn Rockelman, who helped me come up with Aunt Lorna's character during a delightful brainstorming session. They're awesome and zany and crazy, and I love them both.

Any list of thank-yous would not be complete without mentioning my agent, Wendy Lawton, and my editor, Kathleen Kerr. Ladies, you are extraordinary! And my deep gratitude goes to the entire Harvest House team for their work on the Goose Creek books. I wish I could list each of you by name, but believe me when I say I thank the Lord for your efforts.

Here's a confession: I was so busy with "life stuff" that I bumped up against the deadline for finishing this book. I called upon an amazing group of women authors for prayer support as I struggled to meet the date I'd committed to—and I did it with one day to spare. Thanks to the Girlie Chilibeans for their encouragement, email support, and prayers.

Finally, special thanks to Lord Jesus, who has mercy on me even when I let things go until the last minute. As Bach concluded when he was satisfied with a piece of music he'd just finished, *Soli Deo Gloria.*

If you've enjoyed this book, I really do hope you'll let me know. Visit the Contact page at www.virginiasmith.org, where you can send me an email or find the address to send a real, honest-to-goodness letter.

Virginia Smith

# About the Author

Virginia Smith is the author of more than two dozen inspirational novels, an illustrated children's book, and 50 articles and short stories. An avid reader with eclectic tastes in fiction, Ginny writes in a variety of styles, from lighthearted relationship stories to breath-snatching suspense. Visit her at www.VirginiaSmith.org.

✳

To learn more about books by Virginia Smith
or to read sample chapters, visit
**www.harvesthousepublishers.com**